pubs & pegasi

A Cozy Fantasy

Tales from the Broken Claw
Book One

don jones

donjones.com

for the bartenders who've poured so much love for us over the years…

…at Hennessy's
Alecia, Giselle, Isabelle, Kalayann, Kat, Kaylene, and Timi

…at Ice Bar
Carlos and Jen

…at Triple George
Kristy, Marty, and Todd

Here's to you all.

also by don jones

stories of witchkind®

<u>Age of the Adherents</u>:

Daniel Scratch

Master of the Tower

The Fifth Axis

<u>The Order</u>:

The Order of Some

The Conspiracy of One

The Truth of All

———

Clara Thorn

Clara Thorn, the witch that was found

Clara Thorn, the witch that fought

Clara Thorn, the witch that won

———

Endless Sky®

Truthsayer

New Worlds

———

Tales from the Broken Claw

Pubs & Pegasi

———

The Never: A Tale of Peter and the Fae

———

Find more at DonJones.com

contents

acknowledgments

Many thanks to Jim Topp, who has kindly, accurately, and ruthlessly corrected my many ~~tpyos~~ typos over the years, along with, in three books, my terminology for music theory. Any remaining errors are, of course, entirely mine.

Maximum huzzahs to McKenna, who provided the lovely portraits of my characters as well as the cover art.

As always, much love to Christopher, my perpetually patient alpha reader and plot point ponderer.

And of course, many thanks to Travis Baldree for formalizing the "cozy fantasy" genre in my mind. *Legends & Lattes* is a forever favorite.

Urwald
Darkehame
Darkescore Forrest
North Pointe
Common Towne
Gray Foal Pass
The Mistral Mountains
Strongfast
Elgindam
Lake Evendiam
Celestrum
Smallhaven
Scintas
Demonbane Range
Westhold
Lake Midton
Holderdown
Magefell
Skyreach Range
Stormport
Salten Sea
Kithwellen
Lake Trenton
Flameheight Range
Trenton
The Mountedives
Dunereach
Highseat
Shorehaven
Farreach
The Forbidden Continent
Bright Islands
Amber Sea
N

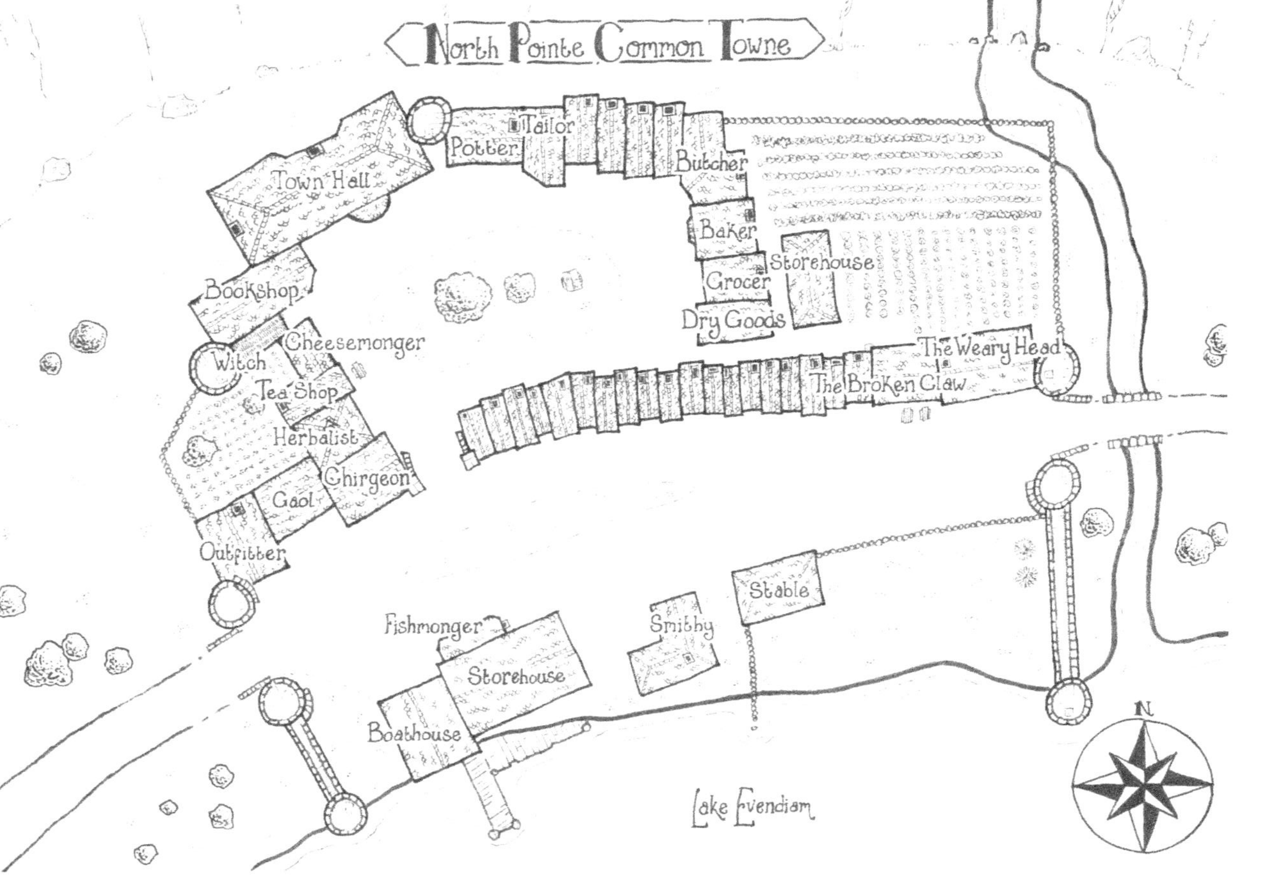

North Pointe Common Towne
Town Hall
Potter
Tailor
Butcher
Baker
Storehouse
Grocer
Dry Goods
Bookshop
Witch
Cheesemonger
Tea Shop
Herbalist
Chirgeon
Gaol
Outfitter
The Weary Head
The Broken Claw
Fishmonger
Storehouse
Boathouse
Smithy
Stable
Lake Evendiam
N

one

. . .

SAM'S HORSE trudged gamely along the wide, hard-packed dirt road. It had been a long day: she'd risen with the sun, packed her minimal camp into a saddlebag, and set out. Hersin, her horse, had gotten used to the routine, but after two sennights of riding, the poor old boy got pretty weary as the sun edged its way into the East.

She'd tried to plan this trip to include more stops in small towns and villages, where she could spend a night in a real bed and Hersin in a real stable. But the lands south of the Mistral Mountains were poorly mapped, especially around Great Lake Evendiam, where she was now. Human habitations came and went, often starting as safe and decently resourced stopping points for a band of travelers. They'd put down roots and form a settlement, which would grow into a village, and sometimes even into a small town. But between the harsh winters, the strange beasts that occasionally wandered down out of the Mistrals, and the near-continual raiding, many settlements and smaller villages simply didn't make it. As a result, mapmakers never attempted to document where lodging could be found, which meant she'd rough-camped for all but two nights of the past two-sennight trek.

It had, at least, been a pleasant ride for the past few nights. The road here curved along Evendiam, putting the cool lake breezes of Springtime on her right, and the thick, shady forest on her left. Further on her left rose the tall, cragged peaks of the Mistrals, their tips still gleaming white with the winter's accumulated snow.

She sighed. She'd heard that more villages managed to survive toward the east side of the—

Wait, what's this? she thought, sitting up a little straighter in her saddle.

A tall, sturdy looking stone wall crossed the road ahead, broken by wide wooden gates that were thrown wide open as if in welcome. As she and Hersin got closer, she realized that an even taller stone wall stretched off into the woods, and that the wall continued a dozen or so yards into the lake itself. Thin streams of smoke declared the settlement to be occupied.

Hersin clopped through the open gate, and Sam's eyes, schooled by years in mercenary companies, quickly noted key details. The gates weren't closed often: dirt and leaves had accumulated around their bases, and there were no telltale scrapes in the earth tracing their swing. But even taller stone turrets—perfect nests for archers defending the town supported the gates. Sam squinted as they passed, but she couldn't make out anyone atop the turrets. *Built to be defended,* she thought approvingly, *but they haven't needed to for some time.* Even better.

The trade road ran straight on, bracketed by buildings on both sides that blocked the view of the lake. *Probably helps block the winter winds, too,* she mused. The buildings themselves were made of heavy, sturdy gray stone, mortared tightly together. On her left was what looked like an outfitter's shop, followed by the unmistakable facade of the town gaol. She smiled at that. *I wonder if they get that many criminals, here.* More likely the gaol was a kind of alternate overnight lodging for travelers who'd had a little too much to drink.

The outfitter's shop and gaol formed a continuous building,

and featured a deep overhang that sheltered a raised wooden walkway. She nodded, recognizing that the construction would help mitigate snowfall directly in front of the shops, and likely provide at least some access between buildings, even in the depth of winter when the snows here would drift deep.

On her right was a tall, wide building that extended a few feet into the lake. *Boathouse,* she thought, and nodded again as she passed a fishmonger's shop right next to it. The—

"Heyla, traveler." A raspy voice greeted her, and she swung her head back to the left. A grizzled, older looking woman in battered leathers stood on the decking in front of the gaol.

I'm one to talk about old, grizzled, and battered, Sam thought wryly. "Heyla," she answered, wincing a bit inside at the gravel in her own voice. "Are travelers welcome here?"

The other woman nodded. "So long as they come in peace, stay in peace, and leave in peace," she said easily, her eyes appraising Sam and her horse.

Constable, Sam thought. *Or whatever stands for that here.* "Peace is what I'm seeking, believe me." This woman was giving Sam an odd vibe. Suspicion, to be sure, but that was expected. This was. . . something else. Sam had learned to trust her instincts in these situations, and her instincts were telling her not to rile this stern-looking woman. Not that she intended to, but this constable looked easily riled. *Former merc, if I was a betting woman.* "Any chance of a pub or an inn?"

A perfunctory smile settled onto the constable's face, doing nothing to soften her countenance but helping play the role of polite host. "Of course. Keep on a bit, past the main gates, on your left. Pub's the Broken Claw, the inn next to it is the Weary Head. Staying the night, then?"

"I hope to."

"Stable's on the right, next to the smithy. Smith's boy, Darby, will likely run out as soon as he spies you." She tilted her head a bit, and Sam had the distinct impression that the constable was looking directly into her soul. "You can trust folk here," she said cooly before turning on one heel and stepping back into the gaol.

Good? Sam thought as she urged Hersin onward. What a strange greeting.

Past the fishmonger's was a long storehouse, and opposite that was the town's main gate. Sam's eyes swept the view as she passed. These gates swung inward and also weren't closed much. They opened into a grassy field of sorts, which was surrounded by a long, continual building in roughly the shape of a lopsided rectangle. *It's a fortress,* she realized at once. *Or once was.* The back of the building was the thick outer wall of the village, and each section of the village rose two stories, some a bit more. With enough supplies, the people here could probably hole up for a long time—certainly through a rough winter—and the additional gates on the trade road would give them a formidable defensive advantage. Nestled tightly as it was between the foothills of the Mistral Mountains and Lake Evendiam, an attacking force wouldn't have much room to move and surrounding the village would be all but impossible. Sam picked out the small emplacements on the building's roofs where archers could perch, giving them excellent firing angles on the adjacent forest and trade road, while giving enemies very little to attack.

The unmistakable sounds of a smithy rang out on her right, and just as the constable had predicted, a young boy was dashing out from the adjacent stable. "Take your horse, ma'am?"

Sam nodded and slid from Hersin's back. "Do I need to worry about these?" she asked, slapping a saddlebag.

Darby's expression was one of affront. "Absolutely not, ma'am!" he insisted. "Safest place in the Mistrals. Constable Jen don't allow no crime, here. None at all. Ha-copper if you're just staying a while, full copper for overnight. Copper includes sweet hay, another copper gets hot mash and a rub-down, unless you'd rather see to it yourself."

Sam tossed the boy three coppers as he took Hersin's reins. "Take good care of the boy, he's earned it," she instructed.

"Yes ma'am!" Darby said with a grin as he pocketed the coins. "Pub's just there, the Broken Claw, if you're looking for refreshment."

"Very much so," Sam said with gratitude. She made a cursory attempt to brush some of the road dust from her leather leggings, promised herself a hot bath at the first opportunity, and stepped across the street. The pub and inn were, like the rest of the structures here, essentially carved out of a single building, again with a wide overhang stretching over a wooden walkway. That walkway was deep enough to host a couple of benches and still provide ample room for pedestrians, and a couple more trestle tables sat just off the walkway in the waning sun. A carved wooden sign swinging from the overhang's edge proclaimed this to be the Broken Claw. An image of a stein sat atop the bar's name, and a crude dragon's foot, one claw broken off, arched beneath.

A bell on the door tinkled merrily as she pushed in.

Long habit forced her mind to scan the place almost without conscious thought. A long, worn wooden bar stretched across most of the back wall. A half-dozen empty trestle tables and benches were arranged between it and the door. Along the left wall, a rack of what were hopefully barrels of ale. Shelves behind the bar held bottles and jugs of what were likely more potent offerings. A large fireplace took up much of the the right wall, and a low fire crackled merrily within. A door behind the bar led to a back room. The—

"Greetings, traveler! Welcome to the Broken Claw. How may I serve?"

Sam's eyes snapped to the bartender, standing behind the center of the bar, offering her a warm smile. His hair was an unruly shock of white, and the wrinkles around his mouth and eyes suggested he'd spent a good amount of time wearing that smile. He was dressed in a simple homespun shirt under a heavy canvas apron. His eyes seemed to flick upwards for a moment before returning to hers.

"Ale, if you've a good one. And I wouldn't say no to something hearty for dinner."

"Please, sit," he said, his smile widening. Sam stepped forward and settled onto one of the wooden stools that lined the front side of the bar. "The ale's easy—I work with a brewer in the next town east of here, and he makes me something custom. We call it Dragon's Rest. Pale, cool, easy drinking, but still with a little character." He reached under the bar for a heavy glass stein, and then stepped to the rack of barrels and began filling it. "Food, I don't do. Worst cook you've ever met. But Minnie, who owns the inn next door, makes the best stew that's ever lined your stomach. Happy to go grab you a bowl, if that suits. Copper for both."

"Suits me well," Sam said, her stomach growling eagerly. "It's been more than a sennight of road rations and what rabbits I could take, and if I never see a piece of hard biscuit again it'll be too soon."

The bartender chuckled as he sat the stein in front of her. Again, his eyes seemed to quickly dart up and behind her, and his smile faded a bit as he once again met her gaze. "I'll just grab that stew. Brown bread okay?"

"More than," she assured him.

He stepped through the door behind the bar, letting it swing gently shut behind him. She took a sip of the beer and her eyes widened in appreciation. It *was* good—light and somehow cool, but with a bit of sass to it. It reminded her of fresh spring water filtered through sunlight. She chuckled at herself. *Now I'm a poet.*

The bartender returned with a large bowl of steaming stew, topped by a generous hunk of rich-looking brown bread. Sam's mouth watered immediately at the savory aroma, and she had to force herself not to start pouring the stew directly from the bowl into her mouth. The bartender let her get a couple of bites in, and smiled as she nodded enthusiastically.

"I'm Nathaniel, by the way," he said, stepping back and picking up another stein and began polishing it with a clean white rag. "But please — call me Nate. Everyone does." Once again, his eyes flicked up and down. Sam started to wonder if it was just a tic of some kind.

"Samantha Godsdotter," she replied between bites. "Sam to anyone who knows me."

"So what brings you to our little village?" he asked easily, although his eyes once again darted up and back. "If you don't mind saying, of course."

"Spent the last thirty-odd years as a merc," she said easily. "Most recently with Sasha's Vixens," she added, jerking her chin toward the scarlet badge on her left shoulder. "Our last engagement didn't go. . . well. That's how I got this." With her free hand, she ran an index finger along the twisted, puckered scar that ran from just above one eye into her hairline. "Goblin axe caught me when I should have been paying attention. Managed to jerk back enough to keep it from cleaving my skull in two, but still knocked me out cold. The others managed to drag me back, and the company medic did what she could to set me right. Once I healed up. . ." she shrugged as she took another delectable mouthful of stew. "Decided I'd had enough. Cashiered out and headed off."

"Came in from the west, then? I've heard of the goblin raids on the western kingdom."

Sam nodded. "Stormport brought in a half-dozen merc companies. Little buggers come pouring down out of the foothills of the Demonbane range, and it was our job to beat 'em back."

"And?" Nate asked curiously, his eyes once again looking past her. This time they stayed for a moment before returning.

She shrugged again. "Still going on, really. Goblin King thinks he wants some seaside real estate, and doesn't mind spending blood to try and get it. But they're primitive fighters. Axes and pikes, mostly. Vixens are mainly light horse and foot, but we were backed by Bard's Badgers, and they've got heavy siege equipment. Ballistas, catapults, that kind of thing. Mass of goblins comes roaring out of their caves, and Bard's boys would just hit them mid-mass. We'd pick off the edges. Lather, rinse, repeat."

"So you're off to find your retirement, then?" *Flick.*

"Seems so." She grinned. "Don't rightly know what that looks like, though. I've been swinging a sword since I could pick one up." She felt a cloud pass over her face, and when Nate's smile faded, she knew he'd seen it too. "You lose a lot of people, fighting that long."

He nodded slowly. "Happy to listen, if there's a tale to share."

Sam nodded slowly as she chewed a bit of bread. "Not much of a tale, I guess. But. . . I'd made a good friend, in the Vixens. Incredible swordswoman named Leeta, just a few years younger than me. She'd been a merc her whole life, too. A real. . . a shieldmate. You know what that means?"

Nate nodded. "We get mercs through here now and then."

"She was my left hand, and I was her right. Fought back to back, side by side, for. . . gods, half a decade. Even Sasha said she'd never seen a pair so in tune with each other."

"I sense this doesn't end well," Nate said softly.

Sam set her spoon down gently, and shook her head. "No. Goblins managed to overwhelm us. Just for a moment. We'd already started to move out of their circle. But one pike. . ." She paused, looking down into the half-empty bowl. "It's why I got distracted. They almost got us both."

"I'm sorry." His tone suggested he meant it.

"Thanks." Sam picked up her spoon, but ate a bit more slowly now. "With her gone, I just didn't have it in me to keep fighting." *I felt like I'd lost half of myself,* she added to herself. "But I've been doing it for so long, I rightly don't know what's next. I've just been riding, hoping. . . I guess, hoping something would come up. Maybe some little town like this would need a constable."

Nate nodded silently, and slid another stein of beer up to her. Sam blinked. She hadn't realized she'd finished the first.

"So you'll stay the night?"

"Aye, by preference. Your constable said something about the inn next door?"

Nate nodded. "Minnie's place, yeah. She'll charge you a copper for an upstairs room, but she's empty right now. I'd ask for the bigger room on the ground floor. Half a copper extra, but it has its own bath. Boiler's right overhead, so you'll get the hottest, freshest water you could ask for. And she lays out an incredible breakfast, included."

Sam looked up and saw that Nate's gaze was now locked somewhere above her left shoulder. She turned, but saw nothing other than the pub's tables and door. An ornate clock of some kind hung over the door. "You have somewhere to be?" she asked politely, turning back to Nate. "I can head—"

"No, no, it's fine," he assured her, his eyes snapping back to hers. "I don't get out much during the day, to be honest," he added with a lopsided grin. "Minnie and a couple of the others feed me. It takes a village."

Sam gave him a hard look as she spooned more stew into her mouth, but Nate's expression remained friendly and open.

"I'm actually open pretty late, most nights," he added unprompted. "Once folks start shutting their shops down, this is kind of the unofficial village gathering spot. Haven't had a bard by yet this season, but eventually one will wander through."

"So what's your story?" Sam asked softly, her eyes on Nate's. "Seems pretty far away from civilization."

He chuckled, but his eyes grew sad. "It is at that. I come from Elgindam."

Sam frowned. "Far East, isn't it?"

Nate nodded. "It's a journey, yeah. Grew up there, married my sweetheart. Never had kids, but we got. . . well, we grew old together. All we wanted, really." Sam's heart clenched for what she knew must be coming. "Lost her to the ague." Nate's voice had fallen to something just above a whisper. "Couldn't rattle around in our house anymore. It was. . . *ours,* you know?" He shook himself, and picked up another stein to polish. "So I joined a caravan headed. . . anywhere." His expression grew thoughtful. "Looking for someplace new to fit in, I guess."

"Bit like me," Sam agreed. "And you came here?"

"Funny story," Nate said thoughtfully, his gaze tracking more slowly up and back this time. He seemed to sink into his thoughts, his tone growing a bit distracted. "Caravan stopped here for the night. A lot do, in the season. Constable lets them line up their wagons on the trade road between the gates. Makes 'em feel a little safer. Came in here, obviously. Tough old lady named Greta ran the place, then. You remind me a bit of her," he said, then blushed as he realized how that sounded. "Begging your pardon, of course, you're not—"

"Oh, I'm old," Sam assured him with a smile. "Tough, maybe. Battered, for certain."

Nate gave her a small smile. "Fair."

"I assume this Greta was looking to move on, then?"

Nate nodded very slowly, his eyes once again rising to look behind her, and then falling back to the stein he was polishing. "After a fashion, yeah. We got to talking, she and I, while the caravan master was wheeling and dealing with the locals. She suggested I spend a night here, get a feel for the place. Promised she'd have someone ride me out to the caravan if they left without me. Asked that I come back the next day and talk to her." He shrugged and placed the stein back under the bar, and tossed the rag over one shoulder. "So I did. Next morning, she told me she was. . . well, ready to move on. Like you said. But the village needs a pub, she said, and if I was looking for something new, something far from my old life, this was new and about as far as I could go." He paused, lost in his own thoughts for a moment. "She stayed for a couple of sennights, helped me get a feel for the place. Introduced me around, you know."

"You have a place here, then?" Sam's attention was locked on the bartender now, the last few spoonfuls of stew rapidly cooling in her bowl.

He shook himself and refocused on her. "Upstairs. All the shops here have living upstairs. 'Cept the village witch, I guess. I mean, she does have a bit of a shop downstairs, more of a parlor, really. You know, some tourists—"

"You have a village witch?" Sam said carefully. Magic wasn't always widely accepted in this part of the world—one of the many bigotries she'd observed in these smaller, more isolated communities over the years.

"Oh, absolutely," Nate said, nodding emphatically. "Leota's her name. She's nice. She. . . her magic is why we don't close the gates, much. Seems to keep the bigger critters out. We don't even really get bandits through here. Those that do seem to move on pretty quickly."

"Don't know that I'd cross that constable of yours, either."

"Hah! No, Jen's pretty formidable. Say, you're spending the night?" Nate sounded distracted again.

"We covered that. Copper and a half, ground floor room, hot bath. Good breakfast."

"Right, right." He looked at the bar, and Sam followed his gaze, realizing that she'd somehow emptied the second stein. "Another ale?"

"I think," Sam said slowly, wondering where the time had gone, "I might turn in. Just next door, right?"

"I'll walk you over."

Nate seemed to regain his focus as he led Sam next door. The Inn's entry was cozy, with a fireplace burning happily along the left wall. Sam realized that it probably shared a chimney with the fireplace in the pub, on the opposite side of the wall. Two clean, well-polished trestle tables filled much of the room, and the rich, earthy smell of stew filled the air. The proprietress,

Minnie, stood behind a low counter, humming to herself as she kneaded a large sphere of brown dough. She was a short, round woman with black hair now going to gray, tied up in a neat bun. She looked up as Sam and Nate stepped in, brushed her hands on a towel that was tucked into her waistband, and smiled. "Room for the night then, dear?"

———

"Oh, merciful gods," Sam breathed as she eased herself out of the heavy copper tub. She's stayed in the bath until the water had become tepid, seriously considering emptying it and starting again before finally deciding she was ready to sleep.

The room was, as Nate had promised, extremely comfortable. The sheets were crisp, clean linen, and the mattress was stuffed with feathers rather than hay. Aside from the low bed and the enormous bath, the room offered a small vanity, a bowl for washing, and a polished piece of steel for a mirror. A tiny wood-stove took the edge off the evening chill.

Minnie had pointed out the privy down the hall, told her that breakfast was served promptly at a candlemark after sunup, and wished her a pleasant night. She'd had Darby bring her saddle-bags, along with assurances that Hersin was well-fed and being well cared-for.

Sam slipped into fresh underclothes, and spent a candlemark or so cleaning and polishing her riding leathers. She laid them out on the cool stone floor, slid under the sheets, and, in the way only seasoned mercenaries and civil servants could manage, was asleep the moment her head hit the soft, fluffy pillow.

———

Sam rarely dreamed, or at least rarely remembered doing so, but when she did, her dreams were intense.

She was in an inn or pub of some sorts, perhaps not unlike

the Broken Claw. But the Broken Claw had been empty, whereas this place was full of people. They were smiling, talking, drinking, and eating. A minstrel or bard sat in one corner, strumming a merry tune and encouraging the patrons to sing along. Sam found herself grinning so widely her cheeks ached.

And there was. . . *something* else there. A presence, of some kind, unseen and only vaguely perceived. To Sam, it felt like a warm cloak, fitting snugly around her. She felt safe, protected. . . complete. A warmth filled her chest, a sharp contrast to the chilly void she realized had been there since. . . Leeta. But in this dream, even the memory of Leeta no longer made Sam sad. In this vision, life was the here-and-now, and the past was, however regrettably, the past. The future was tomorrow, something to be faced when it arrived, and joy was being held in the company of friends.

Sam looked down and was surprised to see a half dozen steins, full of cool, golden ale, clutched in her hands. She shook herself and set them down on the table in front of her, to the cheerful appreciation of the people seated there. The minstrel struck up a new song, and the entire place roared with delight as they recognized a bawdy favorite.

Some dreams come and go, and when they're unpleasant ones you're grateful for a fleeting experience. But when they're pleasant, you want to sink into them, to live in their story for as long as you can. Still, they're often gone too quickly, leaving you feeling a bit regretful as your sleepy mind clutches at the dream's last remnants.

This dream lasted all night, and Sam smiled gently as she snuggled deeper under the crisp, clean-smelling sheets.

two

. . .

SAM STRETCHED AND YAWNED, and then sat up with a start.

Bed. Inn.

The smell of cooking bacon wafted into her nostrils.

Right, the inn. I'm safe.

She'd slept more deeply than she'd have thought possible in a strange new place. When rough camping on the road, she'd had to sleep practically with one eye open, always alert for creatures who'd enjoy making a meal of her, for bandits, and for the dozens of other dangers that awaited an unwary solo traveler.

But here. . . she'd *slept*. Soundly and completely.

I dreamed, she thought as the haze of sleep fell from her and the once-vivid dream began to fuzz into a half-remembered impression.

Sunlight trickled in through the room's tiny window, still tinted orange as the sun climbed its way out of the western horizon.

Good gods, I've gone soft, she thought wryly. *I've actually slept in.* She decided to give herself a break, as it was the first night she'd spent in a real bed in nearly a fortnight, and dispensed with further self-scolding. The ale and rich stew had certainly helped her feel comfortable, and even as she stretched one final time and swung her feet to the floor, she realized she felt utterly refreshed.

She'd forgotten what that feeling even was.

She splashed cool water on her face, dressed quickly, and packed her saddlebags.

"Morning, love," Minnie greeted her from behind the counter as Sam stepped into the inn's common room. "Just you and me this morning, unless Nate pops in, so you can have your druthers. I've got fresh eggs, a rasher of bacon, and some lovely bread that's fresh from the oven. Or if you fancy cereals, I've got two kinds, and some fresh milk from Cole's cow."

"Eggs and bread would be magical," Sam said gratefully, easing herself onto a bench.

"No bacon?"

"Fine, twist my arm."

"Hah! You'd not catch me so bold."

"Any fresh water?"

"Right from the lake," Minnie said proudly as she began assembling the meal. "Whoever built this pile of rocks had the presence of mind to run a pipe all 'round it and right into the lake. Every shop and home has a hand pump connected. Something even filters the silt out before it gets to us—I say the witch's magic, but if you ask her about it she just gives you a kind of sly smile and changes the subject. Here you are. Butter? I've a bit left, expecting a wagon in today. But I've also winter preserves, if you prefer apple jam."

"Oh, the jam. And thank you."

"It's my pleasure, dear. Here you are." Minnie came from around the counter and slid a plate of food in front of Sam. The smell hit Sam's nose and her stomach growled happily in anticipation, as if it hadn't just been full of warm, hearty stew from the night before. Minnie went back behind the counter and returned a moment later with a clean, clear glass and a pitcher of the coolest, freshest water Sam had ever tasted.

Sam tapped the glass. "Not used to seeing actual glass in places this size. No offense," she added quickly. "Nate has real steins, too."

"We're a bit fancy all this way out," Minnie said with a laugh. "Honestly, rowdier towns, I'd stick with pewter and wood, for certain. But here. . . we don't actually have a lot of breakage. And our smith, Warren, fancies himself a bit of a glazier and glass-blower. Sort of a hobby for him, when there's no call for metal-work. This is one of his new glasses he made over the winter, figured out a way to mold them so they come out real consistent."

"You seem pretty self-sufficient, here."

"Oh, have to be out here, love, especially in the winters. We all pitch in to fill the storehouses—we've two, you know, one's right behind the inn—and everyone crams their closets and sitting rooms to the ceilings before the first big snows." She leaned over the counter and called, "Trevor! Mind you get that loaf out before it burns!" She turned back to Sam, chuckling. "He's a delight, but at that age so easily distracted."

"Your son?"

Minnie nodded happily. "Aye, just sixteen this past moon."

"You and your. . . husband own the place, then?"

Minnie smiled gently. "No, my Tam passed ten years back, shortly after we moved here. This place had been closed up for a while, and he'd thought to reopen it when we passed through. We got all that done, but he took ill that first winter." She shook her head sadly, but her expression was still bright. "But the folk here took such good care of Trevor and me, we decided to stay on." She tilted her head a bit.

"You don't miss him?" Sam asked quietly.

"Of course I miss him love," Minnie said gently. "But time heals all, as they say. The hurt's not so deep, this long past. And we had such good years together."

Sam ate a few bites in a contemplative silence.

"You'll be moving on today, then?" Minnie asked.

"I should," Sam sighed, scooping up another piece of egg. "I don't know. Your prices are certainly reasonable, you don't seem all that busy, and the room was perfect. I could see myself staying another night, perhaps. I've been rough camping, and I'm honestly getting too old to be sleeping on roots and rocks."

"We'll start seeing more trade coming through now that the snows are well-past. You're heading east?" Sam nodded as she bit off a piece of bread, briefly closing her eyes in appreciation of the sweet apple jam. "It'll be easier going, then. East side of the lake has a settlement every six or eight candlemarks or so. Ten at the most. Bit safer, as you're further and further from the Mistrals as you go."

"You're all right up against them," Sam pointed out. The mountains were well-known for a variety of dangers, including terrifying bands of orcs.

"Ah, but we've got this fine walled village to protect us," Minnie said, a twinkle in her eyes.

"And a village witch."

Minnie nodded firmly. "Leota's a blessing on us all. She found a warm welcome here, I can assure you but. . . well. Not my tale to tell. But we're all very glad she's with us."

Huh. Sam had always been a sucker for a good story, and it was seeming like this village had more than a few to offer.

"—before you go?"

Sam blinked as she realized she'd missed the first part of Minnie's question. "Sorry. Gathering wool. Occupational hazard of the elderly. What was that?"

"Just asking if you planned to stop in the pub and see Nate before you go."

Sam considered it. "Would he be open this early?"

Minnie considered it. "I think you'll find he's there this morning, at least. I'm fair sure I heard him knocking about when I put the last loaf in."

"Then I suppose I will. Who knows, maybe he can tip me off the fence and into staying another night."

"We'd love to have you, dear," Minnie assured her with a wide smile.

————

"Ah, I was hoping you'd stop in," Nate said with a smile as the front door tinkled and closed behind Sam. "Heading out today, then?" His eyes once again flicked upward, directly over Sam's head.

"I'm leaning toward no, honestly," Sam said, stepping up to the bar and settling onto a stool.

"Oh?" *Flick.*

"Well, it's not like I have anywhere to be. And to be blunt, I think this is the first time in a long time I've risen without a crick in my back. Or neck. Or both."

Nate focused on the stein he was slowly polishing. "So you slept well?"

"Excellent. Truthfully, more than excellent. Like a rock. It's been ages since I've slept this late. And Minnie's breakfast was wonderful, just as you promised."

"Good, good." He polished a bit harder, and Sam wondered what the stein had done to deserve such attention. "Any. . . dreams?"

Sam's shoulders tensed and her eyes narrowed. "Pardon me?"

"None. . . I mean, just asking. I didn't mean to pry. It's just sometimes, you know, in a new place, or after a good meal, sometimes I—"

"I did dream, actually," Sam said evenly, her eyes locked on Nate.

He stopped polishing and looked up. "And?"

"I. . ." Sam stopped and considered. Last night's dream was hazier now, in the way that dreams are under the bright light of morning. But the *feeling* remained with her. The sound of song and laughter. The feel of the full steins in her hands. She held her hands up now, turning them in front of her as if they were new. Rough, calloused, and scarred, they'd served her well these many years. They'd certainly gripped more than their share of sword hilts, horse reins, and shield straps. Never a half dozen heavy steins. "It's hard to describe."

She looked back up at Nate, and realized he was staring firmly at some point above her head. She turned slowly, but still couldn't see anything of interest other than the clock above the— "That's an odd clock," she said slowly.

"It's not a clock," Nate said quietly.

Sam turned back to him, and he met her gaze with a tired smile. "Hang on a moment." He walked to the pub's door, threw the bolt, and drew a curtain over the large, thick-glazed window that overlooked the front walk. "Never any customers this early anyhow," he said easily as he resumed his place behind the bar.

"What's this about?" Sam asked, an odd feeling running up and down her spine.

"When old Greta told me this, she beat around the bush for half a 'mark," Nate said, his face again relaxing into a self-effacing, lopsided grin. "But you seem like a pretty straightforward woman. And you don't seem to have any. . . prejudices around magic."

"On the contrary, I'm a huge fan. Sasha had two combat wizards in the company, and they saved our asses more times than I can count."

"Hmm. You might go. . . easy with that information, when you meet Leota. Some history there, I think."

"So what's the bush we're not beating around?"

Nate laughed, although it sounded a bit nervous. "Point. So look, the thing of it is, this pub is magic. The whole village, really."

Sam nodded slowly. "You'd said as much. Your witch's magic —" she stopped as Nate shook his head.

"It's not Leota I'm talking about. I mean the pub itself. Every building here. Every shop, every home—they all have. . . something. Look, see the thing over the door?" Once again, his eyes drifted upwards.

Sam turned and inspected the thing more closely. It was round, like a clock, but it didn't have hands. Instead, its face was divided into four segments by two lines that cut diagonally over the surface. Each pie-shaped segment was painted a different, pale color—light pink in the upper section, a faded green on the right, pale blue on the bottom, and a barely visible yellow on the left. A tarnished, pitted steel ball was mounted in the exact center. "What is it?"

"Part of the pub's magic," he replied softly. "When travelers come in, I greet them. 'Welcome, traveler, to the Broken Claw. How many I serve?'"

"That's what you said to me." She turned back to Nate.

"I know. But. . . usually what happens is the ball there, the one in the middle, it drifts one direction or another. And then I get a. . . feeling. A sense."

"A sense."

"Of where that traveler's destiny lies. Sometime's it's a direction. 'You should head north into the Mistrals,' maybe. Or. . . this is hard to explain. But sometimes I'll just *know* things. Know that orcs were sighted on such-and-such a peak, or that bandits are blocking the road ahead, or that some princess I've never heard of is being held in a tower I've never seen, off to the east and into the foothills." His gaze drifted back up, and Sam thought he looked. . . sad? "If the ball goes into the top section, it's usually some kind of heroic quest. We get a lot of those. The bottom means someone's on something more personal. Revenge, rescue, that kind of thing. The left is trea-sure-seekers. Don't get so many of those. The right is for people who already know where they're headed, but might need some help. Or a warning." He shrugged. "It sounds crazy, I know."

"Rest assured, I've seen crazier."

"You seem to be taking it well."

"So then what," Sam asked very carefully, "did you sense when I came in?"

"That's just it," Nate sighed. "The ball didn't move."

"Which means?"

He sighed again more heavily. "It's what happened when I walked in. It means. . . the pub is telling me you're to be the bartender here, now. I guess maybe I've put it off longer than I should have, but. . . it's time for me to see new things. To move on. And your destiny is to stay here."

"You can't possibly think—" Sam started with some heat.

"Oh, you can leave if you want to," Nate assured her, setting the stein on the bar and laying his rag across a shoulder. "And if you do, I'll stay. For a while, at least. Probably not long. Someone else will come along eventually, now that it's my time to go."

"And you're just going to. . . leave. Over a little ball."

He smiled, and once again Sam thought he looked ineffably sad. "I've learned to trust that thing. Trust what the pub tells me."

"And what's it telling you about. . . you?"

Nate shrugged. "It isn't, really. I just know that if you're here, then it's time for me to. . . you know. Move on." He coughed again.

Sam stared at the bartender for a long moment. "What is this place? Who built it?"

"We don't know. But we think. . . we think it was built to serve travelers. To be a safe place. Someplace they could re-equip. Rest up. Find out where to go next, what to do next. The pub senses their destiny, their direction."

Something clicked in Sam's mind. "And the inn sends dreams?"

Nate nodded. "Especially after you've been in the pub, we've noticed. They're linked. You dreamed about staying, didn't you?"

Sam nodded slowly. "I think so. Yes. And. . . something else." *Warmth. Protection. Completion.*

"Everyone who stays feels that. Cole, he runs the grocery and the little farm just outside the wall, he and his wife are the newest. They came in a beat-up old wagon behind two worn-out old horses, with their five children. Stayed one night in the inn and decided to stay. The space they took over hadn't been occupied for years, but by the end of the season they'd harvested enough vegetables to make the winter a lot more pleasant for all of us. Ask Cole about it. He'll tell you it all came to him in a dream that first night. His wife, Caitlin, she had it too. They didn't even talk about it the next morning, they just asked if there were any open places in the village."

"And does every shop. . ."

"They all have some gift or another. Tyran, he runs the outfitter's you passed on the way in, he always has almost everything you need, even if it's not exactly what you want. And everything always fits perfectly, always works perfectly. Cole's fields produce more vegetables than should honestly be possible, even out of season. And none of it ever spoils."

Sam met Nate's gaze for another long moment. "You're not joking."

"No."

"And the pub thinks I'm its new bartender."

"It's offering. You've got. . . whatever it looks for, I guess."

"Huh."

"You're thinking about it?" Nate sounded slightly surprised. He quickly turned his head to one side and coughed again, more forcefully this time. "Excuse me, bit of a cold."

Sam frowned. Nate's coughs hadn't been the productive cough of someone with a cold. It had been the wet, thick cough of someone with a *problem.* "How long have you had that cough?"

"A sennight. A bit longer. Galhani, she's our herbalist, she's been making me a tea. It's been helping a lot. Truly," he added when Sam's frown didn't relax.

Sam considered. She *had* been looking for a place to settle, for at least a while. With her background, looking for someplace in need of a constable was pretty obvious, but. . . why not a bartender? "I assume 'moving on' means someplace a little warmer? It'd help with that cough."

Nate smiled. "Might be, might be."

"How long have you been here?"

"Twelve years this moon, in fact."

"And. . . how much would you be asking for this place?"

Nate's brow wrinkled in confusion. "What do you mean?"

"I mean, if I buy this place from you, how—"

"No, no," Nate interrupted, shaking his head firmly. "That isn't how it works. We don't own these places, none of us. They just. . . welcome us in. We play a role. We support each other, we help what travelers we can. You're not buying the place."

Sam stared at him for yet another long moment. "You're actually serious, aren't you?"

Nate nodded. "I am. I didn't pay Greta for it, and you're not paying me for it. It's not mine to sell." He paused and let her consider it. "Are you interested?"

"I—you know, I don't have anything else going on," Sam realized. The sound of laughter and bawdy tavern songs echoed in her ears. "So how does this work? I've literally never worked in a pub before, you know."

Nate laughed, and this time it was a full, hearty, genuine laugh. "I hadn't either. Fortunately, the pub itself does most of the work. But I'll stay on for a few sennights to get you settled in. Give me time to. . . gather myself. You know, get ready. I'll introduce you to the purveyors who supply me what we don't produce ourselves. Most of them should be in over the next sennight or so."

"Do you have a horse?" Sam asked.

"Nope."

"Do you want one?"

"Are you offering?"

Sam shrugged. "If I'm to become a bartender and you're to

move on to new things, seems I'm less in need of a horse at the same time you find yourself in need of one."

Nate grinned. "So, a horse for the pub?"

"I suppose so," Sam said, matching his grin.

He laughed again. "We can call it a bargain." The two shook hands across the bar, and. . . *something* coursed down Sam's spine. Something bright and happy, tingling and sharp. *Welcome,* it seemed to say. *Stay.*

"So how do we begin?"

"Well, first of all, I'm going to move my things downstairs and into the inn. If you're doing this, the pub will want you sleeping here from now on. And then I should walk you around and introduce you to everyone. We should have a trade wagon in today, but we're not expecting any travelers."

"How could you possibly know?" Sam asked.

Nate shrugged. "The pub knows."

"Fascinating." She considered. "And how long am I obligated to stay?"

"You're not," he assured her. "But the pub will know when you're getting. . . restless. Ready to go. It'll find someone new."

"Fascinating," she repeated.

"Why don't you get your things from Minnie's and bring them in? I honestly don't have much—I'll get Trevor to help me pack it up later today. But everyone should be up and about by now, and you can meet your new neighbors."

Sam stood. "Okay," she said softly. Then, more firmly, "Okay. Yeah. I'm a bartender now. This is happening." She looked up at Nate and smiled. "Okay. By the way. . ."

"Yeah?"

"What's this place called?"

Nate grinned. "Samantha Godsdotter, welcome to North Pointe Common Towne."

three

. . .

NATE LED her out the bar, off the covered, raised walk that ran
along its front, and through the gates that opened on the
village's grassy common area.

The common area was vaguely rectangular, deeper than it
was wide, although the odd and irregular angles of the buildings
made it seem more organic and less formal. "Looks like they
built this without much of a plan," she noted. But the buildings
looked incredibly sturdy, made of thick, heavy stone. As along
the trade road, the structures were fronted by a deep, raised
wooden walk, which was covered by an overhang that was part
of the buildings' basic structure.

"We think it may have been finished over a long period of
time," Nate said, "Different leaders came along with different
ideas. But as far as we can tell, it's all original—nothing's been
expanded or modified since it was finished."

The main gates swung inward, and the right side was laid
flat against the exterior side of the pub. Nate led Sam to the
right, past a closely spaced series of doors. "Homes, mostly," he
said. "Folks like the blacksmith and his family, who don't live
over their shops. Honestly, a lot of them are empty. That," he
added, nodding to a narrow alley, "goes to the farm. Grocer and

his family run that, for the most part, and there's a storehouse back there."

"And a cow."

Nate laughed. "And a cow. Honestly, she's a machine. Produces milk more regularly than I'd have thought possible, and I know a thing or two about cows."

The remainder of the village seemed to be one continuous structure. Sam followed Nate onto the covered walkway. "Dry goods," Nate said, pointing to the first door they came to. "Kind of a general store, really. Alred runs it with his mate Carolijn. They're plains elves," he added, looking at Sam as if gauging her reaction.

She shrugged. "Met plenty in my time. Good people." She went to tug the door open, but Nate stopped her.

"They're not up, yet. When we're not expecting travelers, a lot of people tend to sleep in. But Cole will be up. He and his kids wake with the sun when it's planting season." They walked along to the next door, which was standing open in welcome. "Cole? Got someone for you to meet."

Cole turned out to be a tall, heavily built man with a bushy black beard, bald head, and prominent eyebrows. He offered Sam his hand and a wide grin. "Welcome, welcome!"

"Cole, this is Sam. She'll be taking over the Claw," Nate said.

Cole's expression seemed to freeze in place for a moment and then he nodded. "Oh, really? Well, that's wonderful. You're, ah. . ."

"Moving on. Time to try something new again," Nate said.

"Of course, of course. Well, you know we'll be sorry to see you go." Something in Cole's tone tugged at Sam, but she couldn't put her finger on why. "You'll stay a few sennights? Help—Sam, was it?—get settled?"

"At least a couple," Nate nodded. "Just taking her on the rounds. Not expecting travelers today."

"No, but Gotham is due in today. I've got a mess of spring herbs for him, and he's supposed to be bringing in some dairy.

Everyone's low on butter, and our poor cow's milk has been suborned entirely for cheese." He grinned and gave Nate a pat on one shoulder. "Good seeing you this morning. And nice to meet you, Sam," he added, shaking her hand again. "I'm sure we'll be friends in no time. Makota's probably into her second bakes of the day already," he added.

"That's where we're headed next," Nate said. "Hi to the missus from me, Cole."

"See you later, Nate. We'll drop by the pub after dinner."

"Please do."

"Now," Nate said quietly as they stepped out of the grocer's and moved to the next door, "you seem pretty open-minded, but I do want to let you know that we have. . . well, a lot of non-human people live here."

Sam shrugged. "Truly don't care. I've met nearly every race on the continent, I think, and a few from across the seas. Not a fan of goblins, obviously, and I'd as soon leave orcs to themselves but everyone else? Bring 'em on."

"Just didn't want you to be alarmed."

Sam raised an eyebrow, but said nothing further. The smell of fresh bread drifting from the next open door told her they were visiting a bakery. They stepped into a room brightly lit with oil lamps and an enormous fireplace. The fire had been carefully banked, and racks of baking bread sent a yeasty scent to fill the room. Someone—the baker, Sam presumed—was just arranging a few loaves. They turned and—

"Oh," Sam said, blinking in surprise.

"Sam," Nate said evenly, "this is Makota, the town baker."

"*Hsst tch mowwt,*" Sam said.

"Oh," Makota said, mimicking Sam's surprised blinking. "You know Fellisi?"

"We had a Fellis chirgeon in the company I was last with," Sam said with a smile. "She taught me a few phrases. I can never quite get that back-of-the-throat growl, though."

Makota laughed, a bright, sibilant sound, as her feline

features crinkled into a smile. Her tail lashed behind her, a sign of amusement and interest. "You did fine for a human," she assured Sam.

"Well don't I feel the odd man out," Nate chuckled. "Here I was worried you'd be startled at seeing a Fellis family."

"You have kits?" Sam asked.

Makota nodded. "Keen and Sora. I've sent them for more flour and sugar from the storehouse, but they'll take their time about it. No pastries today, just loaves of bread. We're going to do some travel-bread this afternoon. I'm sure we'll see some travelers soon enough." She paused, whiskers twitching. "But I didn't catch your name?"

"I'm a boor," Nate apologized immediately. "Makota, this is Sam. She'll be taking over the Claw."

"The—oh." Makota's tail froze for a moment, before resuming a less enthusiastic back-and-forth wave. "I didn't realize you'd. . . that is. . ."

"I didn't either," Nate said easily. "I mean, maybe I was starting to get. . . you know. Ready for something new." He covered a cough. "But you know, I believe I'm looking forward to it. I'll stay a couple of sennights, of course, to get Sam settled."

"Of course," Makota said quietly. "We'll miss you so much, Nate. But, it's nice to have a new neighbor, Sam."

Sam wished for the hundredth time that she understood Fellis body language better. Something seemed. . . off. Unspoken. *But I mean, of course everyone's going to be sad to see Nate go,* she thought. *No reason to jump at shadows.*

"Sam, any day we're expecting travelers, make sure you get here at the crack of dawn for her jelly-filled clouds," Nate said. "They're light, fluffy, and *so* wonderful when they're hot."

"I shall save you one especially, Sam," Makota assured her. "No need to rush!"

"They're better when they're hot," Nate insisted. "Okay, we're just making the rounds. Dardrad in his shop?"

"I know for a fact he is," Makota said with a slight purr in her voice. "I just got some of the last winter venison from him. We're going to make savory pies tomorrow and I want to soak the meat for a while to soften it."

"Oh, that sounds wonderful," Sam said.

"We usually sell them out of the pub," Nate explained. "And I definitely never nick a slice for myself." Makota just smiled, although something about the set of her eyes reinforced the sense of something unspoken in the air. "All right, off we go."

Out of the bakery, right turn, into the next open door. "Morning, Dardrad. Morning, Dalossalda."

Sam's eyes widened in surprise, because both the butcher and his wife were dwarves. Every counter had been lowered to accommodate them.

"Oh, morning Nate. Who's this, then?" Dalossalda asked.

"Sam," Sam answered for herself, giving the couple a small wave. "Is that venison?" she asked, nodding to the long loin that Dardrad was preparing to slice into.

"Highelk," Dardrad answered. "Wrong season for any kind of deer, but highelk follow almost the exact opposite season. Hunter just brought this lass in yesterday."

"This shop's gift is extra special," Nate said. "Every animal somehow breaks down into two or even three times as much product. And these two waste nothing—bones go into stock, they make soups from the—Dardrad, what's the matter?"

Sam had wondered that herself. As soon as Nate had started speaking, the male dwarf's expression had gone cold. "Sharing our secrets with strangers now, are we?" he growled.

"Oh, no," Nate said quickly. "Sam's taking over the pub."

Now both dwarves' expressions had gone flat and unreadable. "Nate. . ." Dalossalda said quietly.

"It's fine, it's fine," Nate assured her. "I mean, obviously we'll all miss each other. But you know. . . it's time. Probably has been time for a while."

The couple exchanged glances, and Dalossalda's expression, at least, relaxed a little. "Well then. Welcome to the village, Sam.

Nate. . . perhaps we can talk on this more a bit later." It wasn't a question.

"Sure, sure. Of course." Sam thought he sounded nervous. "Um. Lucy up yet?"

"Haven't seen her," Dardrad muttered, turning his attention back to his work.

"Okay. Well. . . be seeing you both." Nate led Sam out, closed the shop door behind him, and seemed to kind of slump. "I knew they'd take it poorly," he said quietly.

"Seems like you're well-liked," Sam said.

"It's not that. They both. . . well. It'll be fine. They take a while to warm up to newcomers, is all. They've been here longer than almost anyone." They walked past four more close-set doors. "All homes, and all empty, if I'm remembering correctly." His tone of voice made Sam pretty sure Nate didn't forget things. "This last one is the tailor's shop."

"We're not going in?" Sam asked when Nate kept moving.

"Um. I guess. Prudence. . . she's the tailor. Or seamstress, if you prefer. She. . . can be a little much for newcomers. And she's not a morning person. I'll introduce you later." He peered into the thickly glazed window next to the adjacent door. "This is Lucy's. She's the village potter. But I don't think she's up yet. Kind of a night owl."

They continued their walk, this time passing a set of hefty double doors. "Town hall," Nate said. "Also the schoolhouse, meeting hall—at least when people aren't just meeting in the Claw—recital hall when the kids put on plays, you name it. Good morning, Vamir."

It's like they have one of each, Sam thought to herself as she spotted the telltale pointed eartips poking through Vamir's thick white hair. As the forest elf's head turned to greet them, she noted his elegant, aquiline features, including the high, sharp cheekbones and steeply slanted eyebrows that marked his race. It was impossible to even estimate an elf's true age, but something about Vamir's eyes made Sam suspect he was quite old indeed. He didn't rise from his bench as he said, "Morning, Nate. Morning, Nate's friend."

"Vamir's our bookseller, as well as schoolteacher. Vamir, this is Sam—she'll be taking over the Claw."

One of Vamir's eyebrows arched even higher. "Well. Good morning, indeed, Sam. Off to. . . new adventures, Nate?"

"Yeah."

"We shall miss you."

"Me too."

Just then, children began streaming out of doors all around the village, running happily toward the schoolhouse-slash-town-hall. Vamir rose gracefully from his bench. "Off to spread knowledge and wisdom," he sighed. "Well met, Sam. I'll be seeing you." He stopped and gave her a searching look. "Do you read, Sam? For pleasure, I mean?"

"I do."

The elf nodded slowly. "I've a book I think you might like, then. I'll bring it by the pub this evening."

"I'd like that. Thank you."

"Good morning, then."

"Good morning."

"This next door," Nate said as they continued on their tour and the elf headed the other direction, "belongs to Leota. Very much not a morning person, and she spends a lot of time indoors. I'll introduce you to her later. And this," he said, stepping into the next shop, "is our village cheesemonger. Morning, ladies."

"High morning, Nate. Who's your friend?"

Sam forced her jaw not to drop. The narrow entry to the cheese shop contained a counter running down the middle. She and Nate stood on one side, while the other was tended by three nearly identical-looking women. Each was tall and willowy, with sparkling green eyes and a slight olive tint to their skin. They all had long auburn hair that reached well past their waists.

"This is Rinca, Clethra, and Fennelis," Nate said, pointing to each in turn. "They're—"

"A dryadic thruple," Sam said. "I've never met one. I mean, I met a dryad once, but. . . I thought you didn't like living within four walls?"

"Individuals don't," Rinca agreed, smiling gently. "Three provides us with the comfort we need to leave the forest."

"Although it's hardly far away," Fennelis pointed out.

"This is Sam, by the way," Nate said. "She'll be taking over the Claw."

All three dryads froze, their gazes locked on Nate. "The leaves turn," Clethra said quietly.

Nate nodded. "And it's time for mine to turn," he said.

"You've told Dardrad?" Rinca asked.

"I have. We'll. . . he said we'd talk more later."

"Indeed," Fennelis murmured. "Sam," she added more loudly, "do you like cheese?"

"I love cheese, although I could probably stand to skip out on hard yellows for a while. I've been living in the road for a fortnight."

All three dryads laughed, a sound that put Sam in mind of brooks and streams running under dappled sunlight. "We can definitely do better," Clethra promised. She picked up a long, narrow knife and carved a slice off the wedge of pure white cheese that sat on the counter in front of her. "Try this."

Sam accepted the slice, and bit off a piece. Her eyes widened, and she made appreciative noises as it all but melted in her mouth. It was sharp but clean, somehow refreshing despite the creaminess of its texture. "That's amazing," she said as she swallowed the last of it.

"That's a White Askata," Fennelis said with a smile. "One of our favorites."

"I've heard of it," Sam said with surprise. "But I thought you needed milk from a Derbian goat? You have one here?"

"Our shop's gift," Rinca said with a sly smile, "is that we can make almost any kind of cheese from whatever milk comes to hand. Come by sometime and we'll show you the back room. It's pretty marvelous."

"I will absolutely take you up on that."

"The ladies also provide the pub with cheese to sell to the customers," Nate said. "In fact, I'm almost done with that last one. It went over *really* well."

Fennelis nodded. "That was a Morde Semi-Sharp. Very salty." She smiled. "We figured it would help sell more ale."

"It did," Nate chuckled.

"I think we've half a wheel in the back," Rinca said. "I'll bring it over around lunchtime."

"Thank you."

"Doing the rounds?" Fennelis asked Sam.

"We are."

"We'll come with you," Rinca announced, and the three of them wiped their hands at the same time, sliding knives and towels into drawers behind the counter. "We're due a cup of tea."

The five of them left the shop and immediately turned into the next open door. This was a tiny shop that smelled of herbs and warm water. A small fire was crackling brightly in a fireplace along the back wall, and a trio of tiny tables otherwise filled the space.

"Good morning, Galhani," Clethra said brightly as the three dryads took one of the tables. Nate sat at another, while Sam looked around to see who they'd spoken to.

"Morning, girls, morning," came a voice. Its owner was visible a moment later. "Oh, hello, madame. Didn't realize we had guests."

"*U 'wethrin,*" Sam said politely.

The gnome's thick brown eyebrows rose nearly to her hairline. "My goodness, your accent is quite good. I'm Galhani, village herbalist and maker of teas." She bowed from the waist.

Sam sketched a bow of her own. "Samantha Godsdotter. Sam.

I'll be. . . running the Broken Claw." She watched the little woman carefully.

Galhani's eyes grew shiny. "Nate?"

"Time for new adventures," Nate said cheerfully, trying and failing to cover a cough.

Galhani frowned. "Let me get you some of your tea. Ladies, the flower blend?"

"If you please, Galhani," Rinca said pleasantly. "And Sam here has been on the road for quite some time. Perhaps you'd have some of that muscle relaxing one?"

"I've just the thing," Galhani said, giving Nate another quick look before she hurried off. Sam realized the one wall contained a gnome-height door into whatever was next door.

"That's her herb shop," Nate said, following Sam's gaze. "This was actually a small jewelry shop before Galhani came, but she wanted to make a tea room out of it."

"You'll not find Dexter in," Fennelis said.

"He's our chirgeon. He's just past the herb shop, last door within the village proper," Nate explained. "He's. . . he keeps kind of odd time. Always there when you need him, but otherwise he keeps to himself, mostly."

Sam nodded, replaying yesterday's journey through town in her mind. "So behind that is the gaol, yes? And before that. . . it looked like an outfitter's shop?"

"Tyran's, yes. 'Mistral Adventures,' he calls it. Ah, bless you, Galhani." The gnome had returned with a tray of delicate-looking tea cups, each one steaming. The collective fragrance was glorious, reminding Sam of a meadow in full bloom.

"Let that cool a bit, Sam," Galhani instructed as she reached up to set another cup on the table. "Takes pretty hot water to get that particular blend to steep, but it's worth the wait."

"High morning, all." Sam turned her head at the gravelly greeting, and saw the constable stepping into the room. She sat down at the unoccupied table. "Any chance for something warm and vigorous, Galhani?"

"Spiced red bark tea coming right up," the gnome said cheerfully. She deposited the dryads' cups in front of them and then hurried back through her little door.

"Jen, this is Sam," Nate said. "She'll be taking over the Claw."

The constable's expression hardly changed, but she nodded acknowledgement. "Well and well. Jennifer Darme, village constable," she said to Sam. "But Jen is fine."

"Samantha Godsdotter," Sam replied. "But please, call me Sam." There was a. . . Sam couldn't quite identify it, but the constable was triggering her instincts in some way. Her hackles weren't exactly *up*, but they were certainly watching warily.

"Making introductions, then?" Jen said.

Nate nodded as he sipped his tea. "Just have to take her to Tyran and everyone along the lakeside, now that you're here."

"Mmm. Thank you Galhani," Jen said as the gnome returned with a spicy-smelling tea. "Looks like you've a few miles on you, Sam," she added.

Sam snorted at the bluntness, but she recognized the underlying query. "More than a few. Most recently with Sasha's Vixens, fighting off goblins. That's where this came from," she said, tapping a finger on her scar.

"Got a few of those myself from back in the day," Jen said, nodding slowly. She took a sip of her tea. "Ah, perfectly scalded, Galhani. You're a master. I was with a company called Bettany's Basilisks. Ever hear of it?"

Sam's eyes widened. "Hear of them? They're legends! Bettany's gone though, turned the group over to her second. They're the Bastards and Basilisks, now. Kethry didn't want her name on it."

Jen rolled her eyes. "Kethry was never one for the spotlight. So you took your cashier?"

Sam nodded. "After. . . well, after this, and some other stuff. I lost one too many good friends, I think. I just lost my heart for it."

Jen nodded understanding. "Life of fighting will do that. So if the pub's asked you to stay. . ."

"I'll be staying," Sam said firmly. She was still getting suspicion-vibes from the constable, but maybe that was just a professional hazard. The woman seemed cordial enough.

Jen stared cooly at Sam for a long moment, and it seemed as if everyone in the room was holding their breaths. Then the old constable nodded once, drained her still-steaming tea, and stood. "Well enough, then. Galhani, I thank you again. Nate, ladies, enjoy the morning. Sam. . . I'll be seeing you." And with that, she left.

Sam realized she *had* been holding her breath when she suddenly exhaled.

"She's cautious," Rinca said quietly as she resumed sipping her tea.

"Part of the village's. . . *gifts*," Galhana said in an equally low voice, "centers on the constable. With the right person in that role, we see almost no violence. No raiders, no bandits. Well, precious few. Anyone with a mind to start a fight tends to just keep going, or get what they need and move on."

"She's been here a long time?" Sam asked.

Nate nodded. "Not as long as the Pebbleblades," he said. "Dardrad and Dalossalda," he added at Sam's confused look. "But a long time. Only those two and Knodalon have been here longer, I think."

"And he would be. . .?" Sam prompted.

Nate took a moment to respond, and everyone else seemed to be waiting for him to do it. "Knodalon runs the lakeside storehouses. He's. . . we probably won't meet him, today. Like Dexter, he kind of keeps to himself a lot."

"He's an unusual. . . person," Rinca said thoughtfully.

"I see," Sam said, intrigued. "Well, I look forward to meeting him in time."

"Do you?" Galhana said. "Hmm." She wandered back through her little door.

"Are you finished?" Nate asked, nodding to Sam's tea.

It had just cooled enough for Sam to pick it up, and she quickly drained it. It was *robust,* full of earthy flavors and something sharp. *Mint?* She couldn't quite place it. But it did fortify her, and she felt muscles relaxing that she hadn't even realized were tense. "What do I owe?"

"Ah, we don't use money here," Nate said as he stood. "Not amongst ourselves. North Pointe truly is a *Common* town. Well, village, but same principle. We take care of each other, each to our abilities, and that's that."

"Oh." *I've never seen that work out in the long term,* Sam thought to herself, *but this place isn't exactly a normal village. Maybe part of its magic keeps everyone getting along.* "Off to the outfitter's, then?"

"Yup." Nate led the way out of the tea room, onto the dewy grass of the square, and out of the town's main gate. "Dexter has a door out here as well—makes it easier for travelers who need help quickly, especially if the village's magic is urging them to move along. That's the gaol, of course, and this is Tyran's place."

Mistral Adventures, the handsome carved sign suspended from the overhang announced. Thick wooden doors had been slid aside to reveal a double-wide entryway. Rough curtains were gathered at the edges, and Sam and Nate stepped through into the shop.

"Wow," Sam breathed as her eyes adjusted. Fires were roaring in hearths to the left and right, making the room almost uncomfortably warm. In fact, if the curtains *had* been pulled, it *would* have been uncomfortably warm. But every other square inch of the place was crammed with open shelves that reached to the stone ceiling, and every inch of those shelves was crammed with. . . *stuff.*

"Tyran, you back there?" Nate called as Sam's eyes tried, and failed, to catalog even a fraction of what she was looking at.

"Nate?" came a voice from the back. The sound of heavy footsteps followed, and now Sam's eyes struggled to take in the shop's owner.

Tyran was a *big* man, with a bald pate and a thick, bushy black beard. His bright eyes were nearly hidden beneath equally bushy, black eyebrows. He was at least a head taller than Sam, and she suspected he could reach any item on even the shop's highest shelves with ease. He was powerfully built, but had obviously gone a bit soft with age, including a substantial paunch. "Ah," he said in a booming voice. "Welcome, traveler! Welcome to—"

"This is Sam," Nate interrupted quickly. "She'll be taking over the Claw."

Tyran stopped mid-sentence, his mouth still open as he stared at Nate. "Oh," he said at last. "I didn't realize."

"Figured I'd save you the spiel," Nate said with a grin. "And yeah. You know the pub moves quickly."

"Yeah," Tyran said softly. Then he seemed to shake himself, and his huge grin returned. "Well then, Sam, welcome to the village! My wife, Morgaine, is still upstairs, but I'll bring her by the pub this evening, if you'll be around."

"That's the plan," Sam said agreeably.

"Met everyone else?"

"Calder will still be out on the lake, but we'll stop and see Pavati. Then it's just Warren and Susan. Leota and Prudence weren't out and about, yet. Nor Lucy."

"Saving Knodalon for later?" Tyran asked. Sam thought his smile seemed to lessen a bit as he asked.

"Definitely," Nate sighed. "And Dexter."

"I'll have Morgaine see if she can't at least get Emma to come with us this evening."

"That'd be nice. I'd like to. . . you know. Let her know."

"Of course. Well, we'll see you then. Sam, wonderful meeting you. Again, welcome to the village!"

"Thank you," Sam replied as she and Nate turned and

stepped back out. The cool morning air was almost a relief. "Is it always that hot in there?"

"No, he just gets it going in the morning and then lets it go. This time of year, at least. But he does like it warm."

"So his spiel—the whole 'welcome traveler' thing—is that part of his shop? Like with the pub?"

Nate nodded as they crossed the trade road. "His shop is the most obvious, actually. The stuff on the shelves will literally rearrange itself when someone comes in. I mean, I don't know if that's *why* he's so boisterous, but it helps kind of cover for it."

"And you said it has anything you might need?"

"Emphasis on *need*, yeah. If Tyran tries to sell you a sword, you damn well better buy the sword, whether you think you want it or not."

"Fascinating."

They walked past the back wall of the enormous boat house, and stepped into the little shop that sat next to it. The space, Sam realized as she took it in, must have been carved out of the larger storehouse space. The interior walls were wood, rather than stone, and a narrow wood staircase led up to what Sam assumed was the family home.

"Morning, Nate," the woman behind the counter called. "Oh, hello there, madame! Welcome to—"

"This is Sam," Nate said quickly. Sam grinned. "She's taking over the pub."

The woman—Pavati, Sam assumed—blinked a few times, much as Tyran had. "Oh," she said at last, gamely adopting a cheerful smile. "Welcome to the village, Sam."

"Do all of you have a 'welcome traveler' spiel?" Sam asked, her grin widening.

"Oh, that," Pavati said, her face reddening slightly. "The— Nate, I assume she knows?"

"She's met everyone who's up, and yeah."

"So our shop doesn't demand it, but everyone else along the

trade road does. Calder started doing it just to fit in, I think. This isn't actually a village shop, if you take my meaning."

"Seems like it was kind of carved out of the storehouse," Sam said.

Pavati nodded. "Exactly so. And so we take advantage of its gift, which means nothing here ever spoils and we have no problems with pests. And Calder catches enough fish that we can salt them and sell them to travelers, which brings in a little money for the village."

"I meant to ask about that," Sam said. "If you don't mind?"

"What we do with the money, you mean?" Nate asked, his lopsided grin returning.

"Basically."

"We have to buy quite a bit from outside the village," Pavati said. "Nate's beer, things like milk and eggs, flour, that kind of thing. Cole's cow is prodigious, but she can't supply us all, let along the girls for their cheeses. So we all pool what we make, and use that to stock up on whatever we need. And there's always hunters to pay for game, or bards or minstrels that we want to stay a few nights."

"Makes sense."

"Do you—" Pavati began, but she was interrupted by a shrill cry from upstairs. "Oh, drat. That's my Dayr. He's six and he's always getting into something. Excuse me," she said, hurrying to the stairs. "Sam, wonderful meeting you, we'll see you again soon!"

"Thank you!" Sam called.

"Good luck, Pavati," Nate added. "They've got four," Nate explained as he and Sam left the shop. "The others are old enough to help Calder on the boat, but Dayr was a surprise baby."

"Big family."

"Biggest after Cole's five."

"Wow."

"Free labor," Nate grinned. "Come on, the smithy will be the last stop." Already, Sam could hear the *clang clang* of metal being hammered. "Warren's been making horseshoes like they're going out of style. He usually goes through a hundred or so every season. Ho, Warren!"

The smith's back was turned toward them, one arm raised high with a hefty-looking hammer gripped in his hand. He brought the hammer down with a mighty *clang,* and then set it down on the anvil before he turned to them.

"Oh, my," Sam said, taking an involuntary step backwards.

"Ogre no eat pretty lady!" the smith roared, holding his arms out wide.

"Oh, for pity's sake, Warren," Nate said with a chuckle.

"Kidding, kidding," Warren said, wiping his hands on his thick leather apron. "I mean, I definitely won't eat you. You must be Sam." He held out one enormous—green—hand.

Sam stepped forward and did her best to give it a respectable shake. "I am."

"Taking over the Claw, I've heard."

"She is," Nate said. "Word finally got around?"

"Susan spoke with Minnie this morning. She's back over there now, taking measurements. One of the upstairs beds is creaking something awful, she said, and Minnie wants to talk about having a replacement frame made up." He peered down at Nate. "Time for new adventures?" Nate nodded silently. "Well. Guess we always knew the day would come. We'll miss you, of course."

"I'll miss you all," Nate said his voice suddenly thick.

The ogre nodded once. "Sam, wonderful to meet you. I'll see you tonight for drinks."

"Good meeting you," Sam replied. "See you tonight." As she and Nate stepped out of the smithy, she added, "Is everyone coming for drinks tonight?"

"They will tonight," he said, his tone still subdued. "But there's always a few who come by most nights, once they close up their shops and have dinner."

"Nobody eats in the pub?"

"Oh, sometimes. Minnie's stews and soups are legendary. But the ones with families tend to eat at home most nights. But once the nights are a bit warmer, folks will throw picnics in the square. The Pebbleblades will do a barbecue one night, Calder and Pavati will do a big fish fry one night, that kind of thing. It's pretty social, really. If we have a lot of travelers in, then everyone has to mind their shops and. . . you know. Play their roles. But when it's slow, like it is tonight, they'll come out."

"Gotcha."

"Ready to move your stuff in?"

Sam took a deep breath. "Yeah. Yeah, I think I am. Let me go grab it from the inn."

four

. . .

"HELLO, TRAVELER," Sam said brightly. "Welcome to the Broken Claw! How may we serve?" Her eyes darted up to the indicator over the door, where the metal ball was already drifting into the"personal tragedy" territory. *Stay,* something whispered in her ear.

She'd been working alongside Nate for a full two sennights now, learning the ins and outs of the pub, getting to know her new neighbors, and most of all greeting and serving the steadily increasing flow of travelers and adventurers that passed through the village.

The latest arrival was a human couple, male and female, probably half Sam's age. No kids to be seen yet, but some people were hesitant to bring younglings into a pub before they scouted it themselves. The two looked careworn and more than a little dusty. Unprompted, one of Sam's hands began reaching under the bar top for two steins.

"Something cool," the man said wearily as the two fell onto barstools. "But not too strong, please. We've a long way to go, yet. Just needed to stop and give the horses a rest."

"I've just the thing," Sam promised. "We've a wonderful, simple small beer in the back. I'll be right out."

Stay, the pub's soft, ethereal voice murmured as Sam stepped through the door behind the bar.

"I got it," she muttered back.

This back room wasn't much: A set of sturdy shelves held some back stock and supplies, while a rack of half-barrels full of small beer, root ale, and ginger bark infusion occupied most of the rearmost wall. A narrow set of stairs on the left led to Sam's compact apartment, while a door to the right led to a back room of the Weary Head next door. A final door led outside into the small farm that sat behind the pub and the inn. Sam quickly filled the two steins with the pale-yellow small beer—always ice-cold, thanks to the pub's gifts—and returned to the front room.

"Here you are," she said. "Copper for both. If you're hungry and can spare another copper, I can get you both a bowl of the best split-pea soup you'll ever have. If you need some snacks for the trail, I've got hard cheese, some cured meats, and a brown bread that should last you a day or two."

Staaayyyy. . .

One thing at a time, Sam chided in her mind. She didn't know if the pub could hear her thoughts or not, but she'd grown accustomed to replying to it. Nate had never mentioned the pub speaking to him in half-heard words. In fact, when she'd told him about it he'd looked surprised. "Always came to me just in. . . feelings. Huh. Might just like you better!" he'd mused.

"Thank you," the woman said with a sigh as she pulled her stein closer and took a sip. "Oh, thank you. Little gods bless you, this is just the thing."

Little gods, Sam said to herself. These folks would be Hillkin, then. "You all from the east, then?" Sam asked. Known for their hard work ethic, large families, near-total sobriety, and a complex and intertwined pantheon of deities.

"Aye," the man replied as he took a deep draught of his beer. "Small Haven, though I doubt you've heard of it."

"Most of my adventures kept me more to the west," Sam said agreeably. "Always heard it's lovely country, though." The pub's front door tinkled again as Nate stepped in. He raised an eyebrow in question, and Sam answered with a tiny, quick shake of her head. He nodded and stepped behind the bar and into the back room. At first, he'd stayed with her when she was dealing with travelers, but in the past few days, as she'd grown more and more confident, he'd been letting her handle things alone. "So what brings you all the way to Lake Evendiam?"

The couple exchanged tired glances, and they managed to look even more downtrodden than when they'd stepped in. "We've kin west of here, up Gray Foal Pass. Haven't heard from them in. . . well, too long. We've been fostering our two nieces, and they're. . ." His voice caught in his throat and he stopped and stared at his beer.

Sssttaaaaayyyy. . .

"You know," Sam said slowly, a strange, vague feeling creeping up and down her back, "the road west of here is a bit washed out. Crews are working on it—nothing major, but we had some hard rain the past few days." The man snorted and nodded, still staring at his beer. They'd likely been riding through the edge of that storm. "Well, it might make the most sense for you to just spend a night and let those crews finish up, is all." The woman's expression turned hard. "Definitely not trying to extort you," Sam said quickly, giving them her best smile. "In fact, given your hardship, I'd be happy to speak to Minnie next door at the inn. I'm sure we can find something reasonable."

"We're not poor," the man muttered under his breath.

"Of course not, didn't mean to imply otherwise," Sam said soothingly. "Only Gray Foal is still a few days off. If you're in need of supplies, I can help you rustle up what you need, and we'll make sure you pay a fair price, is all." A glance up confirmed that the device over the door had settled. "And if you've been riding hard all this way, your horses might benefit from a night off. Darby, the stable boy, loves horses more than his own family, I think," Sam added reassuringly. "They'll be in good hands."

As if to support Sam's argument, a peal of thunder boomed outside, and the pitter-patter of rain on the roof picked up again.

"That tears it," the woman said firmly. "We'll stay. I'll see to rooms," she added, moving to push her stool back.

"Wouldn't hear of it," Sam said quickly. "You relax here, and I'll see to it. And how about that soup? I'm Samantha, by the way. Proprietor here. Sam, to my friends."

"Thank you. . . Sam," the woman said, her expression relaxing a bit. "And yes. Two bowls of that soup would be wonderful. My husband and I can share a room, obviously."

"And I'll make sure there's a hot bath included," Sam promised. "I'll be back straightaway."

Sam stepped in the back, only to find Nate waiting there for her, leaning easily against the stair rail. "Well?" he asked.

"Family headed west to check on their kin in Gray Foal Pass."

Nate frowned. "Road's in pretty rough condition still, and with the rain—"

"I think that's what the pub had in mind as well. They'll stay until morning. They—" a faint tinkle announced the arrival of more guests. "Could I chivvy you into a room and bath for them? Best rate Minnie has, they're tied in knots for worry. Two bowls of soup."

"I live to serve, milady," Nate said with his lopsided grin.

Sam rolled her eyes and returned to greet her new guests.

———

Although the Hillkin couple retired not long after sunset, after nursing two small beers for most of the late afternoon, Sam wound up keeping the pub open until fairly late. The weather remained miserable, the light patter of rain turning into a thunderous downpour around suppertime, and continuing well into the night. Most of the villagers had turned up, hurrying to close the pub's door behind them as the winds from the lake whipped the rain sideways under the broad overhangs. The storm had gotten nastier and nastier as the evening wore on, and Sam had let everyone out the back door and into the garden, saving them at least a dozen or so wet, muddy strides to get back to the shops and homes.

Now she was snuggled in her own bed. The apartment over the pub was far smaller than she'd expected, with most of the pub's second level taken up by a large storage space. But as a merc, Sam had lived with far less for most of her life. Here, a small wooden dresser, a private water-closet, and even a diminutive hand pump for fresh water felt like palatial luxuries. Her little iron wood stove was cold, but the heat radiating from the stone wall—through which ran the chimney shared by the pub and inn—kept her more than warm enough.

A new oil lamp, something she'd purchased from one of the many traders that plied the trade round around the lake, shone steadily. It was an indulgence, but she'd settled into a pattern of reading before she went to bed, and wasn't about to risk her eyesight any further than she already had at her age. Her current selection was the one Vamir had promised to her when she'd first met him. She was only halfway through *Way of the Divided Star*, but she'd found it far more interesting than she'd originally expected. Far from her usual fare of battle tales and fantasies, the book was a philosophical treatise of sorts, positing the existence of souls that were too large to be contained in a single body. This philosophy, the author argued, explained why some married couples seemed all but joined at the hip, thinking and acting with one mind and irritating others whose relationships weren't so close. For Sam, the book reminded her of Leeta. The way the author described two minds working as one, two souls feeling as one, the idea of two bodies somehow acting as one. . . it made Sam sigh with both sadness and a kind of resigned nostalgia. The current chapter proposed the idea that some of the world's most powerful workings—critical battles, legendary magic spells, even incredible meals—could only have been completed by people who shared that kind of deep, highly personal connection.

Sam read for a full candlemark before turning the oil lamp down to a bare glow, setting the book aside, and sinking into deep, dreamless sleep.

———

Her eyes flew open.

A life of mercenary habits doesn't fade in a few sennights or even years, and Sam's eyes and mind raced to assess her situation without her conscious thought. *I'm home. I'm safe. There's no fire. It's false dawn.* She frowned as she swung her legs out of bed, stood, and began dressing quickly. *Something's wrong, though.* She clambered down the stairs, out of the pub, and into the—

Warren was up as well, and already running west toward the far gate. "What's happening?" Sam called as she fell in beside him.

"Nothing good," he said grimly.

Torches were being lit ahead, bathing the area just inside the village's western gate in flickering orange light. Caught between the brightness and the shadows it cast were two wagons, each drawn by a pair of disheveled, panting horses. The rain had given up some time in the wee of the morning, at least, although it had left the trade road a muddy, sodden mess.

Jen was already in the street, calling out firm instructions in her commanding voice. Horses were being unhitched and people were making moves to—

"Sam, Warren," the constable ordered. "Get the backs of the wagons open. Don't touch the people inside."

Neither Sam nor Warren questioned those orders, although Sam's head snapped to one side as the chirgeon's door slammed open and a man Sam had yet to meet—Dexter Walsh, she presumed—hurried out, angling for the rear of the wagons.

One wagon's flat tailgate was already down, but the other was jammed. Warren simply set his jaw, grabbed the top plank of the tailgate, and *yanked*. Metal snapped as the tailgate fell off and landed in the road with a loud *splat*.

"What happened?" Sam asked anybody who might be listening.

"Road washed out," a weary man's voice replied. Sam turned to see what must have been one of the wagon drivers. "Caught an entire caravan." He swallowed heavily, shaking his head. "This is all we could get out. Lake claimed the rest."

Sam's eyes flew quickly across the two wagons, realizing that there were less than a half-dozen people lying under tarpaulins, all of them coughing weakly and struggling to move.

"This one first," the chirgeon ordered, pointing to one of the soaked, injured people. "Into my shop."

"I've got it," Warren said, reaching over the side of the wagon and gently scooping up the individual the healer had indicated.

"Get the rest of them dry, as quick as you can," Dexter instructed as he followed Warren back to his workplace.

Sam clambered into the back of the other wagon, carefully peeling back a tarp. A teenage girl had been huddled underneath, and she gave a low moan as the sodden tarp was tossed into the road. Someone tossed Sam a thick woolen blanket, and she began tucking it around the girl. "You're safe now. I'm Sam. You're safe. We'll get you fixed up. Where does it hurt?"

The girl simply moaned again, shaking her head as she managed to pull the blanket tighter around herself.

The next candlemarks passed in a blur. The entire village had turned out to help, and by the time the torches had burned down the sun was peeking over the mountain tops to the west. None of the people in the wagon had suffered anything more serious than a broken arm, leg, or rib, and even those, Dexter explained, had been clean breaks with little blood. All were suffering from hypothermia, and Galhani had been scurrying back and forth, keeping them all supplied with hot, warming teas and infusions. The village's children had turned out as well, making themselves useful by exchanging blankets, running for whatever supplies the adults needed, and even just holding the hands of the exhausted, shocked travelers who'd almost been washed into the cold, unforgiving waters of the lake.

Finally, everyone had been made comfortable. Limbs were splinted, bellies were full of warm herbs, hair and faces had been cleaned as best as they could, and everyone had been settled in between the two roaring fires of Mistral Adventures.

"Sam," Minnie called from the covered porch of the Broken Claw, "come help me with some food for these poor people!"

Sam nodded and loped off toward the inn. She stopped just short of the entrance as the Hillkin couple stepped out, their arms laden with trays and baskets of simple, hot food. "We'd meant to leave after all, last night," the man said in a low voice. "Seemed a waste to just. . . lay here, in a bed, when. . . we didn't know. But. . ." he paused, and Sam followed his eyes to the two wagons that still blocked the trade road at the far gate.

"That could have been us," his wife murmured.

"It wasn't," Sam said with a sigh, relieving them of some of their burden and leading the way back down the road. "It wasn't you."

They trudged through the soggy road, wiping their boots as best they could before stepping into the bright warmth of Tyran's shop. He and his wife Morgaine—a woman equal his stature—were tending to the injured people, wrapping them in fresh, clean blankets and making sure they had plenty of water.

"Tyran," Sam called. "We've got—"

"Misha?" the Hillkin woman said, her voice suddenly raw. Sam turned, and Tyran managed to grab the woman's baskets before her hands simply fell away. "Matsu? Is that. . . is it you?"

"Aunt Shan?" asked the the teenage girl that Sam had first helped.

It took only moments for everyone to recognize each other, although it took many more minutes for the teary, relieved greetings, and the—exceedingly careful—hugs to wind down.

"So I take it you know each other?" Tyran asked, amusement coloring his voice.

"This is our family," the Hillkin woman—Aunt Shan—said, her cheeks tear-stained but her eyes bright and happy. "My brother, Pol, and his wife Aric," she said, indicting two of the adults. "Aric's sister Natal. This are my nieces, Misha and Matsu. And this—" she paused, looking at the last man.

"Klatu," the older man said, nodding. "We haven't seen each other since you were knee-high to an orc, Shan."

Shan's eyes widened. "Uncle Klatu!" she cried, and the tears and hugs began anew.

"Why were you all on the road?" Shan's husband, who'd been introduced as Adan, asked. "Why haven't we heard from you? Ahme and Robyn, they've been worried sick with—"

"Bandits," Pol said, shaking his head slowly. "Or warlords, to tell truly. Marched into our village one day and announced we owed them all liege and tax. Kicked the headman and his wife out of their home, settled themselves in. Set the kids to working all day, never mind their letters and numbers. Killed the message-runner next he came." He shook his head again. "A bunch of us finally managed to get out. We had one of the big caravans, a bunch of wagons, as many horses as we could manage. Got them all deep in their cups and then lit out at moon-dark. Drove their horses off into the pass to slow 'em down. Rode like the eleven devils was on us." He fell silent.

"How many?" Sam asked quietly.

"Four families," Aric said in a choked voice. "We knew the roads were bad up in the Pass, but we figured once we hit the lake road—"

"It's been storms for days," Morgaine said sadly. "Crews been out shoring up what they could, but—"

"It came out of nowhere," Misha said in a hollow voice. The

girl's hands were wrapped tightly around a large ceramic mug that was still steaming. Galhani, standing next to the teenager, patted her gently on one shoulder. "It was like a wall of water."

Sam turned as someone stepped into the shop behind her. "Came down one of the ravines." It was one of the men who'd driven the wagons into town. He shook his head sadly. "Comes with no warning. Just roars down like a dragon made of water. Cut across the road, pushed everything in its way straight into the lake. Winds were so rough—we couldn't even send anyone in."

"You'd have been killed," Jen said firmly as she joined them in the shop. "Sun's up. You're all alive. Hold on to that. There'll be a tomorrow for all of you."

"We'll go to Small Haven," Shan said firmly. "We've plenty of room. And no bandits, or warlords, or whatever. You'll be safe with us. With family."

Nobody protested, although the woman's pronouncement did bring another wave of tears and hugs.

Sam and the other villagers stepped outside, leaving the family to their grief and relief.

"More travelers today?" Jen asked quietly.

Sam "listened," then shook her head. "I don't think so. Doesn't feel like any pressure to open the pub."

"I suggest you do anyway," the constable said, her low voice raspier than usual. "More'n just those Hillkin folks will need the Claw, today."

———

"Well, that was depressing," Cole said as he sipped his ale.

Nate, sitting next to him, shrugged. "Or hopeful, if you choose to look at it that way."

"How so?"

"That family, at least, found each other. They're safe. They're headed to a safe home."

"Mistrals are dangerous," Dardrad said gruffly. "That's hardly news. 'Specially in storms. You get out alive. . . well, that's a win."

This was the first night the dwarf and his mate had spent any time in the pub since Sam had officially taken over, and she felt oddly relieved at what felt like an overdue gesture of acceptance.

The village had emptied of travelers before the sun set, and despite Minnie's pleas that everyone stay the night and set out in the morning, the clear, crisp evening air had seemed to spur everyone on. Warren had managed some repairs to the battered wagons, and the whole village had helped them stock up on basic supplies for at least the first few days of their trip—particularly Calder and his family, who'd loaded so much salted fish into the wagons that Warren had felt the need to bolt extra metal supports to the undercarriages.

Once the wagons had clattered down the rapidly drying road, a few of the villagers had trickled into the pub, which Sam had wisely unlocked a candlemark or so earlier.

"Mark my words, at least a third will turn out," Nate had said quietly as he helped Sam polish glasses. "The dryads take more comfort in each other, but for everyone else. . . a candlemark or so in the Claw helps them know they're *home*. That they're where they belong."

"Part of its gift?" Sam had asked.

Nate had merely given her one of his lopsided grins and nodded.

Now, with a third of the village indeed gathered around the pub's trestle tables, steins of ale and small glasses of liquor in front of them, Sam could see that he'd been right. Nobody here was drinking just to drink, and certainly not to get drunk, or to forget, or to drown their woes, or any of the other things that usually went on in a pub. Tonight, the village's residents—even a few of the older children, who were quietly sipping malt beer —were here as *family*.

"Made any progress on the book?"

Sam started, then smiled as Vamir leaned onto the bar next to her. The elf could move in utter silence when he wanted to, and she hadn't even noticed him walk into the pub. "I have," she said softly as the other villagers' conversations continued. "About halfway, actually."

"And?"

"It's. . . interesting." A smile played about his thin lips and she chuckled. "I'm serious. It really is. The notion that some feats can only be accomplished by a soul that's too big for one body. . . I don't know. I like it. There's a symmetry to it, maybe. Or maybe it's being part of something bigger, but not in the way the priests are always selling it."

Vamir nodded slowly. "The *Way* is less about serving and more about doing things as one. It can still be selfish, but it's. . . hmm."

"Selfish together?" Sam asked with a grin.

He returned the expression. "Just so." He glanced around the bar. "Planning to stay open late, then?"

Sam ran her gaze slowly across the tables, then shook her head. "No, it doesn't feel like it. I think everyone needed to. . . feel something. Look at Tyran there," she said, nodding toward the huge man. "He was pretty shook up but now he's back to normal."

"Hmmm."

"You disagree?"

The old elf smiled. "On the contrary. I think you should get in there with them." He slid a stein of ale in front of her—one she hadn't even seen him pour. "Go be with family."

Sam stared at the stein for a long moment, and then, with a grateful smile, pulled it closer. "You know, I think I will."

five

. . .

SAM AWOKE MORE SLOWLY the next morning, but her brain still ran through its accustomed checklist. *Warm. Safe.* She smiled to herself as a new item was added: *Home.* Something was poking at the back of her brain, though, and it took her a few minutes to realize what it was: an urge to be downstairs, opening the pub for the day. *Travelers are due, then.* As the spring wore on and the weather grew milder, traffic on the trade road was picking up. As a result, nearly every villager woke early and felt an urge to get their shops ready for the day's custom.

Sam stretched, washed her face, dressed, and headed downstairs. The nudge to open the pub wasn't strong, meaning she'd likely have at least a couple of candlemarks before anyone came rolling into town, which also meant she'd have time for a pastry.

Several of the villagers were particularly early risers: Minnie was always up a candlemark or so before sunrise whenever she had boarders, preparing the morning's breakfast. Cole and his family were usually up at sunrise, puttering around in the farm behind the grocery. Calder's family tended to put their boat out on the lake well before sunrise, ensuring they were over the deeper waters by the time the sun came up and the fish started biting. And Makota was *always* up before the sun when travelers were expected. Her mate, Masaaki, would already have a fire stoked and banked in their enormous brick oven, and with any luck a first round of succulent pastries would already be cooling on racks.

Sam stepped out the pub's back door, waving to Calder's wife Caitlin, who was indeed supervising two of their children in the morning weed eradication. Sam squinted a bit to try and identify the kids, and decided it was probably the youngest, Ivy and Daisy. The others would be inside then, either arranging and inventorying things in the smaller storehouse or in the shop itself, neatening the shelves and sweeping the floors.

Sam turned left down the narrow alley that led to the village square, and then stepped up onto the covered walkway. She inhaled deeply, smiling as she caught the yeasty scent of warm bread and the sweet, light aroma of cooling pastries.

"Morning, Sam!" Makota called as Sam stepped through the bakery's open door. The Fellis' tail waved lazily back and forth as she arranged fresh pastries on the paper-lined shelves that ran along the shop's wall. "Feels like a busy day, no?"

Sam nodded as she scanned the shelves. "It does, now that you mention it. I need to see the ladies about another wheel of cheese, I think." The corners of her mouth dipped a bit in disappointment when she didn't see any of the fluffy, jelly-filled "clouds" that she loved so much.

Makota hissed softly, a sound Sam had come to recognize as a chuckle. "I've a fresh batch of clouds just cooling in the back," she said, her tail swishing more quickly in amusement. "Do you prefer pear or redberries?"

"Redberries," Sam said, grinning. "Am I that obvious?"

"They're everyone's favorites," Makota said. "I've been making a batch just for us, along with a couple to sell. In fact, would you like me to have Kene run a tray down to the Claw? If you're planning to have your doors open before the first travelers arrive, she can sell them off one of the tables out front. She's been dying to help out, and this is the first season she's been old enough to make change correctly."

"Absolutely. And I promise not to eat too many of them myself."

"Hah! We'll just put some insurance on that by filling you up before then. Sora!" she called into the back. "Wrap up a couple of the redberry clouds, and one of those cheese tarts as well. That'll make you a nice breakfast," she added to Sam.

A few minutes later, Sam walked slowly back to the pub, happily munching one of the warm clouds. She'd never run across pastries like these: golden and crisp on the outside, but full of air and melt-in-your-mouth dough on the inside. Wisps of redberry jam threaded throughout the interior, adding a sharp sweetness to every bite. It'd be difficult indeed not to purloin another one from Kene's tray.

When she arrived at the pub, she was delighted to see Nate speaking with Loran, the eldest son of the brewer who made the pub's signature ale. "Ah, Sam!" Loran called as Sam stepped through the front door. "So good to see you! Mind helping me get the empties out?"

"Absolutely," Sam said, finishing her berry cloud and licking her fingers. "Fancy one of Makota's finest?" she asked, offering the bag to the strapping young man. "And there's a cheese tart in there as well, Nate, if you're interested."

"I'd never say no," Nate grinned as he accepted the bag. He fished out the pastries and passed one to Loran as Sam turned back into the pub.

The arrangement with the ale barrels was pretty ingenious, and Sam had marveled over it when Nate first explained it to her. It consisted of a rack that held up to four barrels on top, with room for four more below. All but the end barrel on the top row were empty, and she served out of that end barrel. When it was empty, she simply rolled it along the rack, and a clever chain-drive mechanism let her lift a fresh barrel from the lower row to the upper. At the moment, the full barrel was very full indeed, having just been lifted up a couple of days prior. That left just one full barrel on the bottom, with three empties on the top. Sam walked to the near end of the rack and slid a ramp out from beneath the top row, laying its end on the smooth stone floor of the pub. This made it easy to begin rolling the empties off of the top row and out the pub's wide front door.

"Got it," Loran said through a mouth still full of berry cloud. He'd already laid a similar ramp from the edge of the raised walkway and into his wagon, and he began rolling the first empty barrel up and in. They repeated this for the other empties, and then Loran slid the ramp over to the row of full barrels. These required a bit more care so that they didn't come rolling down too quickly, but Loran had been doing this since he was a teenager, and he maneuvered the heavy barrels with practiced ease. Once one was on the walkway, Sam rolled it into the pub, slotting it into the lower row of the rack. Nate watched approvingly as he munched the cheese tart.

"That should hold us for a moon or so," she said as the last one thumped into its place. "What do I owe you?"

"The usual," Loran said with a smile. "Four silvers apiece, so twelve total."

Sam went behind the bar as Loran and Nate followed her in. She carefully counted out the sum in coppers—the pub didn't see much trade in the more valuable silver coins—and pushed them across the bar top. Loran scooped them into a small leather bag without bothering to count them. "Expecting a busy day?" Loran asked.

"Should be," Sam nodded. "Mornings have been getting warmer, so the trade's been picking up. Lot of folks will have set out a few candlemarks before first light, so they should get here a couple."

"Well, let me get my wagon out of the way, then, and leave you to it."

"Feeling like you've settled in all the way?" Nate asked as Loran walked out.

"I do," Sam said after a moment's consideration. "You know, I never expected it to. . . I guess feel so good. Having a routine like this, I mean. Even when we were just on a patrol job, you never *wanted* it to feel routine."

"How so?"

She shrugged. "Routine meant not paying attention. Not paying attention meant not being ready when something happened. We always rotated people between patrol routes, and we always changed the routes themselves every sennight. Kept everyone on their toes. So you never felt. . . you know, *settled.*" She sighed. "But you also never felt *settled,* and now that I do. . . I like it." Nate covered a cough, and Sam frowned. "That still with you?"

He nodded. "Although it's gotten a lot better since the weather warmed up."

She nodded slowly, watching his expression carefully. "You thinking of moving on, then?"

"Oh, I expect I will soon," he said with a slight nod. "Feels like it'll be the right time."

"Will you hitch up with a caravan?"

"Could be," he said a bit distractedly. Sam could see he was a bit lost in thought, but then he shook himself back to the present. "You know, I've stopped getting *feelings* from the pub. You really expecting a crowd?" He sounded a bit sad.

"Everyone is. Makota's got enough bread and pastries to feed an army, and she's even sending her littlest over with a tray to sell from out front. Oh! That reminds me. I need to see the ladies about getting another wheel of cheese to sell."

"I'll run over," Nate offered, finishing off his tart. "I must have slept weird, because I've got a crick in my back that refuses to go away. I'll go the long way 'round and see if it works itself out. Just one?"

Sam examined her sense of the pub and nodded slowly. "One should do. That hard yellow always sells well. I can always send you for another one if it looks like we'll sell out."

"Reduced to running errands," he said mock-seriously, shaking his head and grinning. "Off I go, then."

————

We actually might sell out, Sam thought happily as she wrapped another large chunk of cheese and passed it over the bar. The day's travelers had started rolling in a candlemark earlier than she'd expected, and the village was *busy.* The trade road was lined with wagons and caravans on both sides, leaving a narrow passage open for traffic to pass. The pub had been so busy she'd been relying on Minnie to run bowls of thick, rich stew from the inn, and Nate had appointed himself table busser and cleaner. She'd left the doors thrown open wide in welcome, and just as one customer left another two walked in. "Greetings, travelers," she said cheerfully. "Welcome to the Broken Claw! How can we serve?"

Her grin grew wider as the device over the door indicated *Heroic Quest.* It was her first, and she gave Nate an excited glance. He grinned back and gave her a quick thumbs-up.

"Two ales, please," the man on the left said politely. He was the younger of the two, clean-shaven, with his long brown hair tied into a neat tail. "And would you have any fresh fruit? I'd kill for an apple."

"I don't, but you won't have to go far or kill anyone," Sam chuckled. "Just head in the main gate, and keep to your right. Grocer's already open and I know for a fact he's got a bin of the best apples you'll ever have. Two ales coming right up. That'll be a copper."

His companion, an older man to judge from the gray creeping into his neatly trimmed beard, smiled back as he slid a copper across the bar. "Any chance that bread I smell is real?"

"Real as can be," Sam said as she pulled two ales for the men. "Just past the grocer's, in fact. And I've stew here if you're hungry for that, there's a fishmonger across the road outside, and we can also supply you with cheese, dry goods, almost anything else you might need. Where are you headed?"

"Gray Foal Pass," the younger man said in a grim tone.

Sam quickly schooled her expression. "Relatives out that way?" she said carefully as she slid the steins across the bar and collected the copper.

"Nothing so pleasant, I'm afraid," the older man said. "There's a bit of a warlord—a thug, really—who's set himself over a village."

Sam raised en eyebrow. "And you're heading off to. . .?"

"We're Elysian Rangers," the young man said proudly. "We're going to free the village."

Sam's other eyebrow joined the first. Elysian Rangers were as renowned as they were rare. She'd met *one* in her entire life, and that was more than most people ever would. They were legendary for their fighting prowess and their dedication to justice.

Sword, the pub finally whispered to her.

"Well, I consider myself honored," Sam said, meaning it. "But. . . just the two of you?"

"This is Elgin's Mission," the older man said, nodding to his companion. Sam could hear the capital *M*, and it means this was the younger man's graduation test before he fully entered the Elysian order. She'd heard the stories of those Missions—always handled solo, although the older Ranger would be grading his charge.

"I see," she said with a nod. "That being the case, if you've need of any equipment, or any supplies at all, really, we've that dry goods store just inside the gate on your right, and there's an outfitter's just down the trade road, past the gates." She cleared her throat. "It would be worth your while to at least stop in the outfitter's and see what you might find useful. Tyran's the proprietor, and he's seen a thing or two."

The older Ranger met her eyes and held her gaze for a long moment before nodding slowly. "You never know what we might find," he agreed quietly.

"Declan, I don't think—" Elgin began to protest.

"You never know," the older man repeated, turning his gaze to his younger companion, "what you can run across in these little, isolated villages."

Like an enchanted sword to help you on your quest, Sam thought. She had little doubt that Tyran's shop would indeed have one by the time these two men got there.

Sword, the pub agreed softly.

"We thank you," Declan said, finishing his ale in one long swallow. "We'll be sure to stop back in if our travels bring us near again."

"Please do. Gods' best on you," Sam said.

"And you," Declan said gravely, nodding. "Come, Elgin. Let's see what we see."

Nate's eyes followed the two men as they left. "Rangers?" he asked Sam softly as he came over and wiped down the bar.

She nodded. "Off to that village in Gray Foal Pass to oust their self-proclaimed new master."

"Never had a Ranger through here," Nate mused. "Where'd you send them?"

"Tyran's."

"Oh." He knew as well as she did what that meant: the village had something it wanted the Rangers to have on their quest.

"Yeah." Sam's gaze turned back to the door. "Greetings, travelers!" she said, shaking off the somber mood as a man and woman stepped in from the road. "Welcome to the Broken Claw! How may we serve?"

———

The rest of the day passed without incident, and without another Heroic Quest. Most of the remaining travelers just needed some encouragement along their way, or a bit more in the way of supplies than they'd been planning to buy, or a nudge to visit the bookshop, or a suggestion to see the herbalist for their weary bones. As the sun began to set in the east, more decided to spend the night safe within the village, heading to the Weary Head to book a room for the evening. A bard passed through, and much to Sam's regret the pub insisted he move on rather than staying and providing a few nights' entertainment in exchange for room and board.

As the last of the visitors either moved out or headed to the inn, a few of the villagers wandered in for a drink. Sam cut up the last chunk of hard yellow cheese and set it out on a board, along with a few slices of rich brown bread, so that people could have a quick snack to go with their ale. Galhani and her mate Lara were first in, and Sam pulled out one of the stools that let the gnomes sit at the proper height at the bar. "Long day for you as well?" Sam asked.

Galhani sighed and nodded. "My wrist's about to cramp, if I'm being honest. It's been a while since we've made up that many sachets in a single day. Must have been, what, Lara, four dozen? Five?"

"Five," Lara agreed as she sipped her ale. "We'll need to replenish the narrowroot in the morning."

Alred, the half-elf proprietor of the dry good store, was next in, with his wife Carolijn. "Sold through an entire barrel of dried beans, four bolts of heavy cloth, and more makings of horse tack than I thought possible," he said wearily as they sank onto one of the benches. "Busiest day I can remember in a long time. Sam, that older couple you sent over took the hint—I think they're going to turn back for home and just make up with their neighbors."

"What changed their minds?" Sam asked. The couple had

come in early, and the pub's indicator had pegged them as Personal Tragedy. It had urged them to visit Alred.

"I think they had some sense that it'd be all villages and pubs all the way 'round the lake," Alred said with a wry smile. "I sold them a map. They were already muttering to each other when they walked out."

"Oh, I remember those two," Galhani said, shaking her little head. "Bone-weary, and they'd been in the back of a caravan all day, not even on horseback. Asked if I had anything that would help them sleep through the day."

"Had to explain why that'd be a bad idea, even riding on the trade road," Lara chuckled. "They'd wake up in even more pain for rolling around all limp and drugged up. So that's what drove them out? Arguments with a neighbor?"

"Well, pretty significant argument," Sam said. "But they're empty-nesters and I think they wanted a change of scenery more than anything else."

Alred nodded. "I sent them back west and advised they head to one of the southern towns, maybe on the sea, for a bit. Easier traveling if nothing else, and even with summer coming on the nights up here are still pretty chilly for bones that old."

Everyone nodded in sympathy, and Sam took that as a reminder to add another log to the low fire she'd maintained all day. The nights *were* pretty cool, although she'd managed to avoid burning anything in her little wood stove upstairs by keeping the fire down here warm all day.

The dryads joined them, sipping honey nectar from small wooden cups, and the conversation soon turned to the evening's tasks and everyone's expectations for the following day. Galhani and the dryads seemed to get a better read on the next day's expected traffic than anyone else, who usually didn't get any sense for it until they awoke. The consensus seemed to be that the next day would be busy, but not quite as hectic as today had been. Before long, everyone had excused themselves and headed home to prepare dinner.

Nate was wiping down the last of the tables and Sam was walking over to pull the doors closed when the constable stepped into the pub. "Evening, Jen," Sam said. "Pull you an ale?"

"Mmm," the older woman said, scanning the pub. "Sure. Nate, how're you doing?"

"Good, good," Nate said. Sam heard him suppress a small cough as she drew a stein of ale for the constable. "Any troubles today?"

"Couple of arguments over rights of way in the road. Expected it, as much traffic as we had today. Nothing more than loud words."

"Here you go," Sam said, placing the stein on the bar.

The constable examined it for a moment, and then finally reached for it and took a swallow. "Good as always. Fresh barrel?"

"Last of the last batch. Probably hold me a few more days, if we keep going as we have. Then we'll be into the batch Loran brought today."

"Fine, fine," Jen said distractedly. Then her eyes snapped to Sam's. "You settled in?"

Pretty intense stare for that question, but whatever, Sam thought. "Yeah, I am. Got a good routine going. I'm liking it here."

"Mmm," the other woman murmured, her eyes locked to Sam's as she took a larger swallow of ale. "Guess you'll be staying, then."

"I am."

"Mmm. Fine, fine." She continued staring into Sam's eyes as she asked, "Make your plans, Nate?"

"Soon," Nate said quietly. "Soon, now."

"Mmm. Sam, you'll let me know. If you need anything, that is." One hand vaguely took in the entire pub. "Help, around the place. Not just if people get rowdy. You know."

What? "I, ah. . . of course. Thank you."

"Even just a chat."

"I'd love that."

"Oh?"

What is happening? "Yeah, definitely. I've really come to enjoy talking to folks. Getting to know people." *Why is this so awkward?*

"Ah." The constable finally broke eye contact as she took a long swallow of ale, draining her stein before placing it back on the bar. "Of course. Of course. Fine. Well. Feels like a busy day again tomorrow." She nodded curtly. "Call if you need. . . anything."

"Absolutely. Thank you." Sam watched, confused, as the Jen let herself out and carefully closed the door behind her. "What in the world was that all about?"

"I have no idea," Nate said, shaking his head and leaning on the bar.

"I don't think she likes me."

"What? No, she likes you just fine. Trust me, you'd *know* if she didn't like you. She just. . . takes a while to get used to people."

"Like Prudence, you mean?" Sam had seen the town seamstress just once, when the younger woman had given her a stern, disapproving stare and swiftly vanished into her shop.

"Prudence is. . . complicated," Nate admitted. "But Jen isn't usually so. . ." his voice trailed off and he stared at the pub's door.

"Weird?"

He nodded slowly. "That was a little weird, yeah," he acknowledged after a moment's thought.

They stood in a comfortable silence for several minutes. "Get you another ale?" Sam asked at last.

Nate shook his head. "I think I'm for bed. I need to. . . it's time for me to think about what's next, I think. And I have a. . . strange feeling about tomorrow."

"Oh? I thought the pub wasn't speaking to you as much now?"

He shook his head. "It's not. Nothing like that. Just. . . a feeling." He gave Sam another one of his lopsided grins. "I'll go see if Minnie needs any help cleaning up."

Sam nodded as Nate let himself out the pub's front door, latching it quietly behind him just as the constable had.

He'd never before left for the night through that door.

six

. . .

SAM WOKE EVEN EARLIER the next morning, well before sunrise, although her brain was a bit more laconic about its checklist. *Warm. Safe. Home.* The urge to open the pub was there, but it was coupled with something. . . *off.* Sam examined the feeling as she washed and dressed, but couldn't pin it down to anything less vague than. . . *off kilter.* She walked slowly downstairs, testing a few options to see how they felt. *Pastries?* No, her belly gently rejected the notion. *Eggs?* The Weary Head had been full for the night, so Minnie would have a pan of eggs scrambled and. . . no, that wasn't right, either.

She went through her opening routine despite how early it was: check that all the steins were clean, wipe down the bar and table tops, make sure the benches were properly positioned, prop open the doors. Get a fire going in the fireplace to ward off the early-morning chill. Step out on the walkway and take a deep breath of the cool air drifting in off the lake.

Still not right.

She stood for a moment. Go see Galhani for a tea? *No.* Get another wheel of cheese from the dryads? *Yes, but not right now.* Maybe wait for Nate to come over, he seemed to be enjoying getting to visit everyone in the. . . *No.*

Why do I feel so unsettled? Wait, could this mean she should be expecting trouble from some travelers today? She reached reflexively for the sword hilt that hung at her waist. She'd never needed it, and although every villager probably wondered why she carried a bladeless hilt every day, nobody had asked about it. Would today be the. . . *No.* That wasn't it.

So what is this feeling of—

"Sam."

Sam whirled, snapped out of her thoughts. Minnie stood there on the walkway, just outside the inn's door. The woman's normally cheerful face was drawn and sad. "Minnie, what's—"

"It's Nate."

Sam's heart clenched. A sensation like ice water trickled down her spine and she felt herself go rigid. The feeling of something being vaguely off-kilter clarified itself. *This.* "Minnie. . ."

"I'm sorry, Sam. He passed in the night."

No. Sure, his cough was still there, but it had gotten better. He'd said. . . "He was moving somewhere warmer."

Minnie shook her head, a tear sliding down her face. Sam realized that her eyes were red and puffy—she'd been crying for some time already. "He knew, Sam," she said softly. "We all knew."

"Knew—what are you talking about?"

Minnie walked over and wrapped her arms around Sam, leaning into Sam's chest as more tears came. "Seeing something new," she sobbed quietly. "New adventures. This is what he meant, Sam. I'm so sorry."

Sam's arms curled around the shorter woman's shoulders as her mind whirled. "He couldn't have. . ."

"I'm sorry, Sam."

"I don't—"

"He's off to his next adventure."

———

"Are you okay?" Galhani asked gently.

"No," Sam said, shaking her head. "I'm not. How could he. . . I mean, he seemed. . . nobody *said* anything!" A lance of hot anger burned through her for a moment before she beat it back.

Sam and Minnie had shared a cry, and then Minnie had excused herself to tell the constable. Arrangements needed to be made, ideally before the day's travelers began tricking in. The village had roused itself, and everyone but Sam had seemed to know what to do. For herself, Sam had simply sat on one of the benches in front of the Broken Claw and watched the somber, quiet bustle. Eventually, Galhani had seen her sitting there and come over to sit next to her.

"We all suspected, before you came," the little gnome said gently, patting Sam's knee. "And when the pub chose you. . . well. We all knew."

"I feel terrible."

"Why?"

Sam stared at the horses in the stable yard across the road, and then shook her head gently. "I don't know. I feel like. . ."

"Nate was ready, dear," Galhani sighed. "Truth be told, he was probably ready a full season before you arrived, but he was holding out until the pub could choose someone. We've never not had someone in the Claw, you know. That and the constable are probably the foundation the village rests on."

"He never said."

"He wouldn't."

"Does this mean. . . I'll eventually. . ."

Galhani snorted. "The village isn't a trap, my love. You can leave anytime you want. And the pub will know if you want to, and if you're a little patient with it, it'll find someone. But some of us. . . for some of us, yes. For Lara and I. We've never spoken of it, but we *know*. This is where we'll spend our days, many may they be. Calder and his wife. Their children may move on, once they're grown, but he'll fish this lake until his last breath, and he takes so much joy in it. Jen's heart is here. Her soul. If you told her she could live another hundred years if she left, or just two nights if she stayed, she'd stay."

They sat in silence for several minutes. Finally, Sam asked, "So what happens next?"

"We've a tradition, here," Galhani said. She slid off the bench. "Come. Nate would have wanted you to."

Sam rose in a half-daze and followed the gnome across the road. Galhani led her through the wide passage between the smithy and the stable, toward the lakefront.

The rest of the villagers had gathered there. Calder and his family had left their little fishing boat tied to the jetty, and had apparently spent the last candlemark before sunrise assembling a crude raft. Sam's breath caught in her throat as she saw the bundle of canvas lying on it.

"Everyone decides their own way," Galhani said quietly as they approached the others, "but most of us choose this."

Even Prudence the seamstress and Leota the witch had turned out, one of the few times in the past sennights Sam had seen them. Prudence turned and gave Sam a piercing, disapproving glare and an unambiguous frown before returning her attention to the lake.

Sam was mildly surprised that it was Cole, and not the constable, who spoke.

"Welcome, Sam. This is a tradition most villagers here have chosen for. . . well, as long as anyone can remember. Those of us who don't move on elsewhere. The lake helps sustain us, and so we trust it to take us on our final journey." He paused, and then continued a bit louder. "Nate was a friend to us all. A friend and a guide to nearly every traveler that passed through our gates. He continued the long tradition of the Broken Claw. He saw it through, saw that his successor was settled." He offered Sam a quick smile. "And now we wish him the gods' best on his next journey."

"Gods' best," everyone murmured.

Calder took a long pole and gave the raft a gentle shove. Sam wondered for a moment how they expected it to go anywhere, with the gentle yet firm breeze still blowing off the lake and into the town. . . but the raft drifted steadily toward the lake's far-off center, quickly picking up speed. In moments, it had slipped into the early morning fog that blanketed the lake's calm, smooth surface. Moments later, even the ripples of the raft's passing had faded.

Everyone watched for a bit longer, and then silently turned and made their way back to their shops. "We'll come together this evening," Galhani said softly, patting Sam's leg before she took Lara's hand and headed back. Before long, only Sam and the constable remained at the lakefront.

"Big shoes to fill," Jen said gruffly.

"I know," Sam said quietly.

"Still feel like you belong?"

Sam turned to the other woman. "What do you mean?"

The constable sighed and looked out at the lake. "Not everyone does. Feel they belong, I mean."

Sam considered it. "I thought I did."

"Make certain. This place. . . it's more than a family. We all have to fit, for it to work." She turned and gave Sam an odd glance. "Make sure you fit. Make sure you know you do." Then, with a curt nod, she turned and headed back to her gaol.

What in the four hells was that? Sam thought, confused and slightly angry. *Should I just leave?*

She turned at a sound behind her. Little Darby was saddling up a pair of horses, which meant the inn's overnight guests were already up and preparing to leave. The sun's first rays had already poked above the peaks to the west. The day's business would begin soon.

Sam shook her head and turned back to the Broken Claw.

seven

. . .

SAM'S MIND wasn't on the job. "Greetings, travelers," she said distractedly as a shadow occluded the light coming through the pub's door. "Welcome to the Broken Claw, how may I serve?" She barely glanced at the device above the door, and blinked when the ball slid into Heroic Quest territory. Her eyes dropped to the four men who'd just stepped in.

"Four ales," the tallest of them ordered.

Sam's brain clicked into mercenary mode as she scanned the quartet. Three were dressed as fighters, no question about it: light leather armor not unlike what she herself was accustomed to wearing, well-used swords slung across their backs, knives at both hips, and light but sturdy boots suited to riding as well as moving quickly in a battle. Each had long hair gathered into tight tails, and their faces bore the same scars and weathering that her own had accumulated.

The fourth was cut from an entirely different bolt of cloth.

That one was the shortest of the group, and he was dressed in a severe, heavy, dark-red robe, complete with a cowl pulled up far enough to obscure his face in shadow. He walked with small, efficient steps, and Sam could just make out the glint of the firelight in his eyes as they swept back and forth across the pub.

Wizard, she thought with some trepidation. *And not a good one.*

"Four ales," she said calmly, pulling steins out from under the bar.

"The inn next door," another of the fighters said. Sam nicknamed this one Blondie, the taller one Grizzled, and the third Red, after their hair color. "Do you know if there's room?"

"Full last night, but most folks will be pulling out if they haven't already. You're. . . planning to spend the night?" It was early, yet, the sun barely halfway up the sky. Most travelers would be making the most of the daylight to get as far as they could on their journey.

"We travel by night," Grizzled said, accepting a stein from Sam.

That's not weird or troubling at all, Sam thought as she filled and served three more steins. The three fighters stood at the bar rather than seating themselves, and the wizard stood behind them.

"Should be rooms available as soon as Minnie cleans 'em," Sam said, forcing herself to maintain a neutral tone. Something about these guys was really setting off her base instincts. Past them, she saw Jen walking slowly past the pub's entrance, staring inside. *She feels it, too.*

Potions, the pub whispered to her. *Leave before sunset.*

Sam's eyes widened despite herself. The pub wanted to *help* this crew? "Is there, ah. . . anything else I can help you with?"

"I don't suppose," the wizard asked in a low, grating voice, "someone in this little backwater would have a supply of hallowflower?"

His voice sent chills down Sam's spine, and her skin seemed to tighten. Hallowflower was a well-known herb—well-known because you mainly wanted to keep away from it. As far as Sam knew, it had some legitimate uses for easing severe pains, but only in the smallest, most diluted quantities possible. She'd mainly encountered it as a poison.

Potions, the pub repeated.

You can't be serious, she retorted silently. Aloud, she said, "You know, I don't know that one. But I know who might. Why don't you make yourselves comfortable and I'll go find out?"

"Appreciation," the wizard hissed. Almost as one, the four men turned and settled onto benches at the table nearest the bar.

Sam scurried out.

"What's their deal?" Jen asked sharply as soon as Sam stepped off the walkway and into the road.

"Wizard—a Blood Wizard, if I'm guessing—and three fighters. Planning to spend the *day,* if you will. 'We only travel at night.' And they're asking after hallowflower."

"You're going to Galhani's?" Jen asked carefully.

Sam stopped. "I was thinking of getting *Warren,* actually," she said in a steely voice. "We need to run these guys out before they—"

"That is *not,*" Jen said, grabbing Sam's arm and pulling her to the side of the road, "how we *operate* here. What did the pub tell you?"

"What part of *Blood Wizard* do you not understand?" Sam hissed. "We can't just—"

"We serve all," Jen hissed back, leaning so close to Sam's face that their noses almost touched. "That's the purpose of this place. Of all of us. If they come in peace, stay in peace, and go in peace, we don't put judgments on them. Their destinies are their own. We *do not* judge who the gifts of this place are shared with. *What did the pub tell you?"*

Sam blinked at the intensity of the constable's voice. "Potions. And to tell them to leave before sunrise."

Jen nodded. "I'll go to Minnie and ensure she's got a room free at the back of the inn, away from the road noise. Go to Galhani."

"But—"

"Go. She'll understand."

"Do you even *know* what hallowflower is used for? They're—
"

"I wager I know more than you, actually," Jen said cooly, easing back a half-step and releasing Sam's arm. "If that's truly a Blood Wizard, a hallowflower potion will let him absorb more power from someone's death. Makes it more intense, more painful. That's what they live on."

Sam blinked again, her jaw working furiously. Finally, she managed, "You *know* that?"

"I've run up against a few, in my day."

"And you're *okay* with it?"

"We. Don't. Judge." The constable leaned forward again, her words delivered in a voice that brooked no dissent. "This place, all of it, only *works* if we follow its lead. *Their destiny is not ours.* Do you understand what that means?"

"It doesn't—"

"Is there evil in the world? *Yes.* Do we love it? No. But we are unaligned, here. We *have* to be. It's the terms of this place. You were a merc, Sam. I know the Vixens were pretty selective about their jobs, but are you telling me you were *never* on the wrong side of a fight?"

Sam stepped back. "I mean. . . sometimes there's no right side."

"Exactly. Took your pay though, didn't you?"

"We—"

"That's the job of a merc. You fight for whomever pays."

"It's not the—"

"It *is* the same. And if you can't commit to that, can't understand that, then you put us all in danger." Jen took a further step back and gave Sam a hard, cool stare. "You can't *fit* here otherwise." Her eyes bored into Sam's. "We. Serve. All." She turned on one heel and strode toward the inn.

Sam blinked again, her mind whirling.

Potion, the pub whispered.

Fine, she shot back. Ten long strides took her to the village's main gate, and she stormed into the herbalist's shop.

"Morning, Sam, how's—oh. What's the matter?"

Sam explained.

"Ugh. Thanks for coming over. I'd honestly rather not deal with them directly. But let me get you a pouch. Charge them a full gold for it, mind you, and don't touch the stuff yourself. If he—"

"You can't be serious," Sam said with disbelief.

Galhani sighed. "Right. This is your first one. Look, the rules of the village are pretty simple. We serve—"

"—all, yes, Jen had a word with me on the way over. But—"

Galhani shook her head firmly. "There's no 'but.' If they don't keep the peace, we'll deal with them. But there are rules. Tenets that go back centuries. Further. There's. . . fate in the world, Sam. Destinies. Journeys that have to be taken, stories that have to play out. Not all of them are bright and happy. What if fate *wants* those four to get their poison, to go out, and what if there's some hero out there, whose story is to slay them? What if that's part of that hero's journey, the thing that puts them on the path to some-thing even greater?" The little gnome shook her head as she pulled on a pair of heavy leather gloves and began transferring a slick-looking bunch of leaves into a thin leather pouch. "We don't interfere. This place is *part* of those stories, a place along the way on those journeys. We play our part. It'll turn out how it's meant to. We break that covenant. . . and we lose all this, for everyone. We can't do good by anyone if we're not here."

Galhani finished filling the pouch, tied it tightly, and passed it to Sam. "A full gold piece. Don't open it yourself."

"You're okay with this," Sam said flatly, looking at the death- and pain-filled pouch in her hand.

"No. There's a lot in the world I'm not okay with. But. . . these things have to play out. And it isn't always pretty."

Sam stared for a moment longer. "Did Nate ever. . ." her voice trailed off.

Galhani nodded sadly. "More than once, my love. More than once. Go. Play your role. We'll still come together tonight. We'll talk it through."

A sense of peace slid across Sam's skin. "Okay," she said softly as she turned to go.

Sam walked briskly back to the pub, her mind roiling with conflict. She stepped back into the pub and walked to the table, where three sets of eyes and one cowl tracked her movements. Grizzled stood as she approached the table, and she held the pouch at to him. He accepted it wordlessly, dangling it to one side in front of the wizard. The cowl considered it for a moment before the wizard reached up and, without opening it, stashed somewhere within his robes. "One gold," Sam said. Grizzled cocked an eyebrow, but produced the coin and placed it into Sam's outstretched hand. "Someone's seeing to rooms for you. Back of the inn, away from the noise of the road." She forced her voice to approximate a friendly tone.

"Many thanks," Grizzled said with a nod.

Sam returned to the bar and began furiously polishing steins. A moment later Minnie bustled in through the door behind the pub. "Who'll be wanting the—ah, I take it that's you, gentlemen?" she called. The fighters' heads swiveled to the bar. "If you'll just follow me, then. You can bring the steins, dears." Minnie's voice was as chirpy and cheerful as always as she eased past Sam and led the four men out the pub's front door.

"Wait," Sam called, suddenly remembering. Grizzled, the last one to the door, turned and raised an eyebrow in question. "You might. . . with the roads, and all. Best be moving a bit before sunrise, if you want to make the best. . . time."

Grizzled nodded slowly. "We appreciate the. . . suggestion?"

"Absolutely," Sam said quickly. "Just based on my experience."

"Thank you," he said, nodding graciously before turning out the door.

Sam set the stein down and let her anger lower to a simmer.

She glanced at the fireplace, decided it could go another candle-mark or so, and simply stood, staring at the pub's open door and waiting for another customer.

I wasn't always objectively in the right, was I? she thought. *That time in Kithwellen, even Sasha wasn't happy about the job. But we needed the money. Maybe we didn't end up killing anyone who didn't deserve it. . .* Sam paused, remembering the little villages. The ones who'd been in open rebellion against the legitimate monarch, whose own armies were off seeing to their borders. *Expanding them, not 'seeing to them,'* Sam sighed to herself. *He was a tyrant.* And the villagers hadn't been wrong to want to be rid of him. But he'd been the legitimate monarch. . . *And that's all we needed to take his gold,* she admitted.

Jen stepped into the pub.

"Hey," Sam said softly.

"Hey. Our visitors bedded down?"

"Minnie came and got them."

"You gave them the. . . advice?"

"And the herb. Yeah."

"Want to talk about it?"

Sam thought about it for a moment. "You're not wrong," she sighed. "Four hells, you're actually right. We tried to be choosy about our jobs, but. . . we weren't always on the right side." Jen nodded and waited for Sam to continue. "What do I need to know? What else, I mean? About this place?"

The constable settled into a stool and nodded to the empty stein. "There was a tension in the air, this morning. After. . . Nate, I mean. It's gone now. Fill that for me?" Sam nodded and turned to fill the stein. She slid it slowly across the bar, into Jen's waiting hand. "I've been here a long time. Not the longest, but a long time. Nobody knows much about this place, who built it. Or why. . . it is what it is. It lives on travelers, somehow. On their destinies. On seeing them on their way. On giving them the little pushes, the little jog at the elbow. A magic sword here, some calming tea there."

"You saw the Rangers, yesterday."

Jen nodded. "And saw the sword they came out of Tyran's with." She chuckled and shook her head. "The most rusted-out, pitted, sad-looking sword you'd ever seen. The younger one was *quite* vocal about how much they'd paid for it. But the older one. . . he sensed it. Trusts this place. I've no doubt that sword will be the one to cut down whomever they're after, no doubt it'll be the strongest, sharpest sword that young man will ever hold."

"Yeah."

"Or," Jen continued, giving Sam a meaningful stare, "perhaps it'll shatter at the worst moment, and that young, hopeful Ranger will be killed." Sam's eyes widened. "We can't know. Can't know his destiny, can't know his story. All we can do is. . . trust. Trust that the world as a whole will turn out the way it's meant to. And play our role in it."

Sam considered that, and then nodded. "Yeah."

"So you're okay?"

"Yeah."

"Do you feel you. . . *fit?"*

Sam sighed. "Yeah."

Jen took a swallow of ale and then tilted her head. "I'm sure you noticed this village's defenses when you first rode in."

Sam nodded, and then her eyes widened. "Gods, my horse. I—"

Jen chuckled. "Darby's been learning to ride. That horse has probably never had it so good. You can tell the boy to sell him, if you want, but he's welcome to stay, too. *That's* what came to your mind?"

Sam smiled softly, unconsciously mimicking Nate's lopsided grin. "I'd promised him to Nate. You know, in exchange for the pub. Not exactly, but. . ." she fell silent.

"Ah."

"But yeah, to your point, I did notice that the gates hadn't been closed in some while."

"And we're not exactly awash in archers."

Sam grinned again. "No."

"But we're obviously in an area that's replete with minor warlords, thugs, you name it."

"I. . . well, I guess I'd wondered. Why we're not a target."

Jen shrugged. "I can't say for certain, of course. But I suspect it's because they sense something about this place. They know we're not. . . *in* the world, exactly. We're not an opportunity. We get by, but there's nothing about us that makes us a target. Come in peace, stay in peace, leave in peace. . . we welcome all."

"We serve all," Sam echoed hollowly.

"Exactly."

Sam sighed again, and as she exhaled she felt more than just the breath leave her. Something else went with it. A burden. Something she hadn't known she'd been carrying. Her shoulders relaxed a bit. "Yeah. I get it. I—" Her eyes flew open as a sense of alarm stabbed her.

The constable's expression mirrored her own. "Outside," Jen snapped. "Quickly."

eight

. . .

"LITTLE GODS," Jen breathed as she and Sam skidded to a halt in the middle of the trade road.

Standing at the west gate was an enormous yak-like creature. Thick, gnarled antlers curled upward from its head. White, wool-like fur covered indigo scales. Its eyes, set below a broad, wrinkled brow, exuded gentle red flames that licked at the air. It was *huge,* its head nearly cresting the top of the village's stone walls.

It pawed the ground and exhaled a rush of steam from wide nostrils.

Halfway between Sam and Jen, and the creature, stood Darby. He was facing the monstrous being, and he seemed absolutely transfixed. A horse's halter lay at his feet in the dusty road.

Around and behind the two women, the villagers and travelers who'd crowded the trade road were coming to a slow, quiet stop as they all caught sight of the beast.

It took a step forward, pawing the ground and exhaling another blast of steam. The flames coming from its eyes briefly flickered blue and green.

Darby didn't move.

"That's a Qilin," Sam said quietly. A gentle rasp made her look at the constable, who drew a wicked-looking knife from its sheath. "Don't," Sam urged.

The Qilin huffed and took another step forward. Still, Darby didn't move.

Warren stepped out of his smithy, reaching toward his son. He pulled back when the Qilin snorted loudly and tossed its head, orange sparks flying from its nostrils.

"Warren, no," Sam called softly. The ogre turned to her, his brown eyes wide with fear, but he stepped back. "It's on a mission," Sam added more quietly as she placed a hand on Jen's forearm. "They never come out of the mountains unless they're on a mission."

"Then what's it doing here?" Jen asked through gritted teeth, her eyes still locked on the massive creature.

"It's said they mark the passing of major rulers. Or the coming of one. But. . . they're unpredictable." Indeed, the last time Sam had seen one it had galloped through an entire army, crushing a full battalion beneath its flaming hooves and spewing thick, greasy flames to either side. And that had been the army of the new ruler it heralded—the opposing army had fared far worse. "Darby," Sam called in a gentle voice, "step back here, buddy."

The boy didn't move, didn't even flinch, even as the Qilin took another step toward him.

"Darby—" Jen started to order in a louder, stern voice.

"Get everyone else out of the way," Sam interrupted. "It's going to walk through the village."

"Four hells it is," Jen said cooly. "Not in—"

"It is *going to walk through the village*," Sam said urgently. "This is not something you can control. Clear a path. Get everyone into the square."

Jen waited a moment before sheathing her dagger and taking a step back as she turned to go—but as she did, she leaned and whispered fiercely into Sam's ear. "Know why it's here, Sam. Know why and help it along."

"Know—what do you mean?" Sam asked, confused. Her eyes flicked to the constable.

"The pub, Sam," Jen hissed. Then she darted off, waving everyone toward the main gates.

The pub. The pub where villagers gathered to feel. . . at home. To feel that they were where they belonged. The pub that sensed travelers' destinies, and gave them little pushes and assists.

This is my role. This is why I fit.

Sam closed her eyes and, for the first time, actively tried to *feel* the pub's presence in her mind. She focused on the place in her mind where its voice had always whispered, letting the trade road, Darby, and the menacing, fire-breathing Qilin fade away. "Greetings, traveler," she whispered. "Welcome to. . . North Pointe Common Towne. How may I serve?"

A light grew in her mind's eye.

She felt a sense of urgency. . . of unrest. Of. . . what had Jen said, earlier? A *tension.* Something had been stretched to the breaking point, and it was about to snap. And when it did, there would be a set of strong hands to hold it, to bring it back together. . . or there would not. There was a blockage, a barrier in the way of what *could* be. A wall that needed burning, needed trampling. Birth was painful, change could be even more so, but there was *something* needing to be born, needing to change.

And the way to that something cut directly through the village.

Passage, the pub whispered. *Quest.*

Sam's eyes snapped open.

She took four confident strides to Darby's side, putting her hand on his small shoulder. The Qilin snorted again, more sparks flying from its nostrils. The flames rising from its eyes grew brighter, tinged with bright yellow. "We serve all who come here," she said firmly. "All who come in peace, stay in peace, and leave in peace. Please, let me show you through."

The Qilin's head tilted fractionally to one side, and it pawed the earth again.

Sam steered Darby to one side of the road, where his father's arms wrapped around him and lifted him up, off the road, and into the smithy. Her eyes firmly on the Qilin, Sam turned and gestured along the road, hoping that the constable had been able to clear a path between the wagons lined up along one side, hoping the space was wide enough to permit this gigantic beast to pass. "Please. Be on your way."

The Qilin held Sam's gaze as it began walking—slowly, but with steps so large that the distance between them vanished in seconds. Its head turned and its eyes tracked her until it was directly in front of her, looking down. She craned her head back to meet its burning gaze. It smelled of hot earth and spices, dry leaves and freezing winds.

Sam's mouth was as dry as the deserts she'd served in as she said, "You've come in peace. Stay in peace. We grant you passage. Leave in peace on your quest."

The Qilin paused for a moment, solemnly nodding its head ever so slightly before turning and breaking into a gallop. It was through the town and gone in an instant, leaving a rush of wind and a cloud of hot, parched dust settling behind it.

"Sam—" Warren started to say.

He caught her as she passed out.

———

The few travelers who'd decided to spend the night in the village had taken flagons of wine and ale and retired to their rooms in the inn, mentally exhausted by the day's events. Nearly all of the villagers, even the children, had gathered in the Broken Claw. What should have been a loud gathering, with so many people in the space, was instead subdued.

Sam quietly passed around steins of ale, along with cups of juice for the younglings and small beer for the older kids.

"To Nate," Warren said, raising his stein.

"Nate," the others echoed. Sam's heart was heavy—the day had been so long, and so full of tension and panic, that this morning's goodbye seemed impossibly distant. But already she missed Nate's puttering in the pub every evening, the way he'd mindlessly wipe the table tops after the last customer had left. The way—

"None of that," Galhani said loudly. Sam shook herself and met the gnome's eyes. "We all see you thinking it. That's not what he wanted."

Dardrad cleared his throat noisily. "I remember when Nate first came here," he said in a rough voice. "Dalossalda, do you remember? He was with that ridiculous caravan."

His wife snorted as she took a gulp of ale. "Claimed to be on a tour of Lake Evendiam," she said, shaking her head in amusement. "Why, their next stop was supposed to be for fishing and *swimming,* if you can believe such a thing."

Calder matched her snort. "Lake's never warm enough for swimming," he said. "Bryn can testify to that."

Calder's oldest smiled. "I'd fallen off the jetty the next morning," the boy said. "Nate came running out of the Claw with blankets, insisted on dragging me back in."

"As if our own fire wasn't already warm," his mother grinned. "But that was Nate, wasn't it? Took to the pub like a fish to water. Wasn't even here a day before it was talking to him like he'd grown up here."

"You know, he's the one who told Lara and I about scrimthread," Galhani mused.

"No! Really?" Morgaine said with surprise. "That's my favorite tea! What did we do before then?"

"You drank plain black tea," Lara laughed. "Once we'd gotten that starter root, though, we worked scrimthread into nearly everything. Makes any tea so much. . . warmer."

"Nate helped us clean out the shop," a small, severe voice came from the back of the pub. Sam's eyebrows rose as she realized it was Prudence. Her little toddler, Bryant, was asleep on her lap, nestled against her bosom. "He was the first to make us welcome." Her eyes slid to Sam's, and her lips dipped into the frown Sam was used to seeing. *As if it's my fault he's gone.*

"He was the first to make a stew explode," Minnie said cheerfully.

"Wait, what?" Sam asked in surprise.

Now Minnie was chuckling. "Oh, Makota, you must remember."

The Fellis and her mate were letting out the soft hisses that served as laughter. "It's a pub, Makota, it's got to serve stew!" she said, her eyes bright with amusement.

"I thought you made the stew," Sam said, confused. "Nate said he couldn't cook."

"Oh, he couldn't," Minnie agreed. "And I never used to keep a pot on all day. But the poor boy wouldn't be denied. 'A pub's got to serve stew,' all right. So he sets up a giant pot, just in front of the fire. No idea what he put into the thing."

"A few candlemarks later, we all heard it," Makota said.

"Blew the lid right off it, whatever he did," Alred laughed. "Carolijn ran down straight away."

"Hot stew everywhere," his wife said, tearing up as she remembered it. "Oh, it took us *candlemarks* to help him clean it all up."

"Ruined the pot, too," Minnie recalled. "He must have had that fireplace hotter than the sun itself, had bits of meat and gravy melted right into the metal."

Warren was laughing now. "Oh, I remember that. I melted the whole thing down in the forge and made horseshoes from it. They probably still smelled of it!"

Everyone was chuckling at the memory.

"That's when I offered to keep a pot simmering in my kitchen," Minnie said, wiping her eyes. "Said he could just come get bowls whenever someone needed some."

"That stew was the best meal we'd had when we first came,"

Cole said, shaking his head sadly. "Nate convinced us to stay the night."

"And that's what convinced us to stay," Caitlin murmured. Everyone fell quiet for a moment, lost in their own thoughts.

"Nate served us all," Warren said at last. "He'll be missed."

"He walks new roads," Rinca said. Clethra and Fennelis nodded agreement. "He explores new forests."

"And we welcome Sam again," Makota said firmly. "She who will keep the circle of the Broken Claw intact."

"To Sam," her mate, Masaaki, declared.

"To Sam," everyone murmured, raising their cups and steins. Sam noted that even Prudence took a sip.

"That creature today," Cole said with a sigh. "What did you say it was, Sam?"

"A Qilin," Sam said. "Second one I've seen. That's two too many, by the way."

"You said they heralded. . . a new leader?" Lucy asked.

Sam nodded slowly, sipping her ale. "The coming of a new leader, or the passing of one. Not sure which it was. Scary as the four hells, though."

"With all the little warlords we're hearing about," Leota said from her perch near the fireplace, "perhaps it's the coming of a new leader. Someone who can unite the lake villages. Provide some peace."

Warren snorted. "Be nice if we could at least mount a defense if one—"

"Enough of that," Jen snapped. Everyone turned to her, startled by the sharpness of her tone. "Sorry," she amended. "But you know. . . how it is."

"Actually," Sam said, wondering if it was the ale making her bolder, "I don't. I feel like I have to learn about this place in dribs and drabs. Mystery and smoke. *How* is it, exactly?"

The room was quiet for a moment.

"There's magic on the village," Leota said matter-of-factly. "Obviously. But. . . as near as I can tell, it expects certain roles to be filled at all times. The gaol. The pub. Even their positions in the town. . . they anchor it, somehow. Some roles are. . . flexible. Lucy, we didn't have a potter until you arrived. Never have, as far as I can tell. So the village adapts, so long as every role has something to offer the travelers who stop here. But. . . it won't stand for keeping people out."

"Even evil wizards," Sam muttered.

"Even them," Leota said, raising an eyebrow and taking a swallow of ale. "Every destiny is served here. We don't know why. Even I can't tell. But. . . part of it is that the village isn't *whole*."

"What?" the constable asked sharply.

Leota was shaking her head. "I know, Jen, I know. But it's not. I've been telling you that for a while. *Something* is missing. There's. . . a tension."

That word again, Sam thought.

"Tension." Jen sounded displeased.

"Tension," Leota repeated. "It's. . . testy. It needs something more. And until it gets it, it's going to be testy about keeping anyone out. Even closing the gates."

"Is that why the gates haven't been closed in. . . forever?" Sam asked, intrigued.

"Largely," Leota said, nodding. "There are eighteen of us," she said. "Who hold roles," she added as one of the dryads opened their mouth to speak. "Eighteen who hold roles. But that's not what it wants. There's. . . more. It's hungry for some-one. For something. And it's searching. Everyone who passes through. . ." Leota's voice had become distant now, distracted somehow. "I can feel it looking at them all."

"I've felt it," Warren said softly.

"I have too," Galhani agreed.

"So we *can't* defend ourselves?" Sam asked.

"If we're actually threatened, yes," Leota said. "But not. . . proactively."

Sam looked at Jen, but the constable merely frowned.

"Not until it gets what it wants," Leota said. "What it *needs.*" She gave Sam a long, searching look.

The constable drained her mug and left, shutting the door gently behind her. The conversation resumed as the other villagers remembered Nate. Sam had trouble keeping her eyes off the pub's door, except as they drifted up to the device mounted above it.

The ball remained firmly in the center.

nine

. . .

SAM HAD to pry herself out of bed the next morning. Everyone had stayed up far too long into the morning, reminiscing about Nate. Eventually, the conversation had turned to the fearsome Qilin, and Sam had shared everything she knew about the beasts —which wasn't much. Eventually, probably just a handful of candlemarks before the sun was due to rise, everyone had made their way out, carrying or half-carrying sleepy children who'd been allowed up far past their accustomed bedtimes. Calder, as he'd ushered his sleepy tribe out the door, had firmly announced that there'd be no fresh fish the next day.

Sam's mental need to open the pub was fairly mild, suggesting a slower day of traffic along the trade road, and indeed it was almost noon by the time the first travelers rolled in. They fell into the Personal Journey category, and Sam simply encouraged them to load up on supplies and continue on their way so they'd reach their destination more quickly. The next was a pair of would-be heroes planning to head into the Mistrals to fight ogres; the pub had insisted they seek out lesser opponents, and Sam had done her best to dissuade them with tales of orcs' prowess and near-invulnerability. In the end, she'd made up a story about an enchanted battle-axe, and encouraged the two to seek it out in the forests well to the south.

The third set of travelers was something different altogether.

"Greetings, travelers," Sam said as they walked in. "Welcome to. . ." she paused as her mercenary's mind scanned the group and started raising red flags. ". . .the Broken Claw. How may I serve?" she finished, her voice losing any trace of charm.

These four were *bullies*, she decided at once. Their heads swung back and forth as they entered, not scanning the otherwise empty room for threats as she might have done, but seeking out *targets*. Sam's back muscles tightened as something inside her prepared for action. Her eyes flicked upward as the ball in the device above the door slowly arced between Quest, Treasure Hunter, and Already Knows Where They're Going. *Great.*

"Four ales," one of the newcomers growled, clearly irritated that there was nobody else in the pub for them to bother.

"Right away," Sam said, forcing an easy tone as the four settled heavily on either side of the table nearest the door.

Conquest, the pub whispered. *Scouting.* Sam's eyes widened. *To the west for someone weaker, to the east to gather their forces.* Sam's heart began beating faster. That was the most verbose the pub had been with her. It seemed to be searching the men, looking for something they might need, looking for a way in which to serve them. *East,* it decided. There was a hesitancy behind that, and no suggestions that the four should visit any of the other village shops. *Salted fish,* it finished at last, seeming to shrug and give up. Its attention hovered over the room, as if casting a wary eye on the foursome.

"Here you go, boys," Sam said, letting the rasp in her voice come through as she stepped around the bar and sat four steins on the table. "Hungry?"

"Oh, aye," one of them said, grabbing Sam's forearm. "Any-place in this hole offer something a bit sweeter than you?"

Sam smiled and grabbed his hand, pushing her thumb into a nerve in the man's wrist. He grunted and released her, and she casually made her way back behind the bar. "Not that kind of town, chum," she said with false cheer. "Good place to stock up on supplies, though. Fishmonger's across the street, I can recommend his salted whitefish. You boys heading east?"

"Just came from east," another one muttered.

"Things get a bit dicier to the west," Sam lied. "Whole villages full of fighters. Not so welcoming as us. Back east's easier pickings."

"Pickings for what?" he growled.

Sam shrugged. "For whatever you might be up for. Where'd you boys head in from?"

"Gray Foal—" one began, but fell silent when his companion jabbed an elbow into his ribs.

"Our business is our own," that one said sharply.

"Not my place to pry," Sam agreed easily, picking up a stein and beginning to polish it. "Let me know if you'd like a bowl of stew or some bread or anything." Her eyes narrowed as one of Calder's daughters ran past outside, calling to someone.

Four sets of eyes turned to the door. "Well, that certainly looks a little sweeter," one man said with an evil grin. "You've been holding out on us, barkeep."

He stood just as Jen stepped in front of the pub's door. She was wearing a heavier leather vest than usual, and she'd strapped on leather bracers as well. "Afternoon, boys," she growled in her raspy voice. "Glad to see you settled. Sam here taking care of you?" Her eyes flicked to Sam, who gave a tiny shake of her head.

"This place is a little slow for us," the man who'd stood growled back. He took a step back into the pub as Jen entered.

"Come in peace, stay in peace, leave in peace," the constable said. "Happy to help you find your way out, when you're ready to go."

"What if," the man sneered, "we're *never* ready to go? This seems like a nice, soft place for us, and we could certainly. . . pick up the pace a little."

These four are seriously out of touch, Sam thought. She could feel an ire rising from the pub itself, and from the look on Jen's face, the other woman could feel it was well. Whatever the village normally did to discourage this kind of behavior wasn't working on these four. Sam frowned as she realized all four of them had identical metal badges sewn into their heavy leather jackets—badges intricately worked with arcane-looking symbols. *They're shielded in some way.*

"I try to avoid violence in my town," Jen was saying in a hard voice. "But I use the word *avoid* quite advisedly."

"See, we're just the opposite," the man said as his three companions drained their steins and stood. "We *like* a little violence now and again."

"That's enough, boys," Sam said, stepping around the bar. Two of the men turned to face her. "Why don't we get you resupplied and on your way? Plenty of—"

"Shut up," one of the men facing her said succinctly, taking a step toward her.

A rush of air and. . . *something* blew through the pub. Sam blinked. Jen's right arm was now covered in armor to her shoulder, and a two-foot blade extended from her now-gauntleted hand. "Then let's just get you on your way," the constable said cooly.

The four mean each drew long, nasty knives—short-swords, really—and squared off. *Dreugers,* Sam recognized at once. They'd be wickedly sharp along both edges, and were well-suited for close-quarters combat. Popular weapons in the militant kingdoms to the far east.

The two facing Jen spread out a bit, forcing her to split her attention between them, while the two facing Sam took a step closer together, their weapons held in opposing hands.

Sam's hand dropped to her belt, lifting her bladeless sword hilt from its catch and holding it in front of her. With a *snap*, its blade appeared, shimmering with the reflection of an orange-blue light that didn't come from anywhere in the pub. Across the pub, Sam saw Jen's eyebrows raise, and a grin tug at the corner of her mouth. The other woman's shoulders seem to set, and she leaned forward a bit onto the balls of her feet. A fighter's stance.

Just then, something *clicked* in Sam's soul. In her mind, she was back on the battlefield with Leeta, standing side by side and facing down a dozen opponents. For the first time since that last battle, Sam felt *right*. It was as if a limb she hadn't known was missing was suddenly back in place, flexing itself after long misuse.

"Couple of witches here, then," one of Sam's opponents said, his face stretching into a grin. "What'd we do with the last witch we found, Tomis?"

"I think we gutted her," his companion said. He lunged at Sam, stabbing his blade toward her midsection, just as his companion raised his *dreuger* for a downward slice.

Sam stepped easily to one side, letting the lunging sword slide past her, and brought her own blade down in a chopping motion. It cut easily through the man's sword, leaving him with flat-ended stub of a blade, while the rest of his weapon clattered harmlessly on the pub's stone floor.

His eyes flew wide and he let out a curse as Sam reached out slightly with her upswing, catching the edge of the other man's blade on the flat of her own. The two rang like the peal of a bell, and the man frowned at the casual force in Sam's swing. "We can still keep this civil," she said easily.

"Got your horses all saddled up, boys," Jen said smoothly, stepping back through the pub's door and onto the walkway. "Why don't you just be on your way?"

One of Jen's opponents lunged, and Jen moved in a complicated step-and-back that dodged the blow. The bracer on her left forearm trapped the man's sword against the pub's door frame, while the sword on her right hand flew up to the man's neck. He leaned back, but Jen's arm simply inched forward, keeping the point of the blade *just* against his skin. He'd either have to hold that position or release his own sword.

"Plenty of light left in the day," Sam offered.

"Aye," Jen's opponent growled. "Fine, witches. We'll go."

Jen performed another quick side-step, releasing the man's blade, lowering her own, and leaving the doorway free.

"I'll keep that," Sam said, stepping on the ruined blade that lay on the floor as its former owner made to reach for it. The four men eased themselves out of the pub, not sheathing their weapons until they were off the walkway and in the trade road.

Sam followed, stepping out to the opposite side of the door from Jen. Warren was already standing in the road, holding the reins of four horses. The other few travelers in town had retreated to the opposite end of the trade road, and none of the other villagers were present.

"Four hells, they've got a tame ogre," one of the thugs muttered.

"Ogre no eat nice men!" Warren bellowed, giving the four a toothy grin as he handed them their reins. He stepped back toward the smithy's entrance, crossing his thick arms across his broad chest. "Ogre no eat nice horses!"

The men mounted quickly, wheeling their horses toward the east gate. One of them gave Jen and Sam a nasty look as they kicked their horses into a trot and thundered out of town.

Sam sighed and let her shoulders slump. With a *snick*, her blade vanished and she replaced the hilt on its belt hanger.

"Nice blade you've got there," Jen said, a cold breeze swirling as her own weapon vanished. For the first time, Sam noticed the heavy steel bracelet encircling Jen's right wrist.

"She's named Nailbiter," Sam said with a tired grin. "And I could say the same about yours."

"Hellsting," Jen said with a bit of a grimace at the bracelet. "Not a name I'd have chosen, but she's saved my butt more than a few times. Hate bringing her out like that, though."

"Sure," Sam shrugged. "Keep the peace, and all that."

"No, it's not that. She takes a good bit of my own energy, and I skipped breakfast today." The constable reached around to rub the small of her back. "And I'm not so young as when I first got her," she added with a wry grin.

"You two okay?" Warren said, stepping across the road.

"Yeah, don't know why those two didn't get the usual message," Jen said, shaking her head.

"Shields," Sam said. Jen cocked an eyebrow. "At least, I assume. They all had engraved badges sewn into their shoulders."

"Ah. Yeah, that might do it. I didn't spot those," Jen admitted. "That's a little worrying."

"How so?" Sam asked.

"That kind of magic isn't cheap," Warren said, his brow wrinkling.

"No. Which means someone with means is backing those idiots." Jen looked down toward the east gate and frowned.

"So is that the kind of defending ourselves the village allows?" Sam asked quietly.

Jen nodded and turned back to Sam. "It knew it didn't want any of those four, and if they weren't going to take the hint to keep it peaceable, then yeah. It's okay with us running them out."

"What if they'd pushed the issue?"

Jen stared at her for a long moment. "Hasn't come to that," she said at last. "I. . . don't know. When there's a constable in the gaol there's usually no chance of violence. Those four. . . that's the closest I've come to a real fight since I've been here." She sounded worried.

"You think they'll be back." It wasn't a question.

Jen exchanged a glance with Warren. "I think. . . maybe we should assume they will."

"Ogre bash heads?" Warren said with a small grin.

"If they do come back, they'll come back with friends," Jen mused. "Did they head back the way they'd come?"

"Yeah," Sam said. "From Gray Foal Pass direction."

Jen frowned. "Been hearing that name a bit too many times recently."

"Yeah."

"Let's chat tonight. Maybe we can come up with—"

"What's that?"

Both women turned as Warren spoke. The ogre's head was tilted back, and his eyes were tracking something in the sky.

They followed his gaze and Sam frowned. "What in the four. . ."

ten

. . .

THE THREE OF them ran toward the village's main gates. Already, a small crowd of traders and travelers were gathering there, looking into the grassy village square, their mouths agape.

Warren's mouth joined them as Jen said, "It can't be."

"Gods of filth," Sam cursed.

"Is that a pegasus?" the child of a traveler asked.

The creature that had just landed in the village square, trotted a lap to shed momentum, and then calmly started grazing on the bright emerald grass, was indeed a pegasus. Its glossy black coat shone in the afternoon sun, and its wide, raven-dark wings glistened with highlights of iridescent greens, blues, and purples.

"Disgusting," Sam scowled, earning her confused stares from several of the people gathered at the gate.

At exactly that moment, the pegasus raised its head, stared directly toward Sam, and delicately raised its tail as a half-liquid stream of black-and-green dung poured from its rear.

"Gross," Warren said, wrinkling his nose. Ogres were known to have a highly developed sense of smell.

"And it'll walk around doing that until we get rid of it," Sam said, her lips still twisted in disgust. "And if we don't clean up after it, the whole village will smell like a compost heap. At best."

"Drive it—are you mad, woman?" one of the travelers asked in a shocked tone. "This must be some kind of blessing! For such a magical creature—"

Another fetid pile of feces dropped to the formerly pristine grass, and the pegasus shook itself, furled its wings, and continued grazing.

"'Magical,' my ass," Sam said. "They're a health hazard, is what they are."

"Maybe we can sell the dung," Jen ventured.

"Stuff's no good for planting," Sam said, shaking her head. "Ugh, I can smell it. Nobody'll buy it. Not good for anything except smelling to the heavens and being slimy. It'll kill anything it touches, mark my words." She considered. "Maybe we could put buckets of the stuff on top of the gate turrets. Something to dump on those thugs, if they come back."

"Darby!" Warren called, turning back toward his stables. "Get out here with a shovel and a bucket!" More quietly, he added, "Do you think we could get some of Calder's kids out here to help?"

Sam snorted. "You'll need it. These things travel in herds. Flocks. Whatever."

Jen's eyes widened as she stared at Sam in horror. "You're joking."

"I am not."

"Gods."

"Yeah. I'm going to back to the pub."

Sam smiled at the young couple in front of her—Personal Journey with a hint of Knows Where They're Going. "My scar," Sam said kindly, tapping her forehead, "tells me it'll storm in the next day or so. Why don't you two stay here for a night? The Weary Head, next door, is pretty reasonably priced, and Minnie lays in an amazing breakfast. If you're not in a hurry." *Stay,* the pub had suggested, which meant the two had a date with a dream at the inn tonight.

The two exchanged a quick glance. "We're not in a rush," the woman said hesitantly. "And. . . we were hoping to see your pegasus. If we're allowed." Her eyes were dewy with desire as she turned back to Sam.

Sam's eyes rolled upward of their own accord, but she quickly marshaled them back. "More power to you, although I'd advise taking something to cover your nose and mouth."

"My nose and—why?" the woman asked with a slight frown.

"Because the damn thing craps like a sailor who's drunk too much unfamiliar water," Sam said frankly. "The village kids have been cleaning it up, but I think the novelty is starting to wear off on the older ones. Smell's strong enough to melt your nose hairs, and even with nose plugs I swear you can *taste* it." The couple's eyes widened. "It's fine out here with the breeze off the lake," Sam added with a shrug. "And inside the inn all you can really smell is stew and firewood. Frankly, I'd rather wallow with a passel of pigs. But yeah, if you want to go see it, help yourself. Want me to show you the way?" This late in the afternoon, Sam wasn't feeling as if any more travelers were expected in, and she'd been hoping to close up a bit early.

"If. . . you don't mind?" the young man said.

"Right this way." Sam took a moment to soak a rag in her strongest-smelling grain spirit before stepping around the bar and leading the young pair outside.

Much as Sam had expected, the traders passing through had either heard of pegasi and knew to keep clear, or they'd quickly figured it out. Their wagons were parked along the road as usual, but just inside either the eastern or western gates, instead of further in. A couple had even camped just outside the gates, where the lake breezes were a bit stronger. She nodded to Pavati, who'd tied a scarf around her face as she bartered with another pair of travelers for salted fish. Calder and their older kids had put out before the crack of dawn and announced they wouldn't be in until the last of the sun's rays were catching the clouds. The fisherman had made it clear he preferred the smell of rotting fish to pegasus dung, and his three older children wanted nothing to do with mucking out the village green.

"Oh!" the young woman sighed as she caught sight of the admittedly beautiful pegasus. "It's so—oh." That last syllable was uttered in a markedly less pastoral tone. "Oh, it's. . . strong."

"Ymmf," Sam agreed, holding the liquor-soaked rag over her face and mouth. Alcohol fumes were preferable to the slimy smell that came out of that creature's rump.

"I think maybe this late, we will stay, but. . ."

"In thr imm," Sam agreed, nodding.

"Yes."

"Tl Mmmy m smt mmu."

"Sorry?" the young man asked, already backing away from Sam.

She took a deep, alcohol-laced breath, took the rag away from her face, and quickly said, "Tell Minnie I sent you" before replacing the rag.

"Okay," the two said, turning and hurrying away from the gates.

"No good'll come of it," came a rocky voice behind her.

Sam turned. A grizzled, ancient-looking man sat on a low stool in front of the storehouse's thick oaken door. Reluctantly, she pulled the rag away from her face. "Wait, are you Knodalon?" This was the first she'd seen of the elusive storehouse keeper.

He nodded, grimaced, and spat into the dry earth of the road. "Damn things travel in herds, you know."

"Yeah, I know. I'm Sam."

"I know."

"You've seen pegasi before?"

He spat again. "Used to hunt the damn things, 'cept nothing'll eat 'em."

"Hope you kept your bow," Sam said, shaking her head and replacing the rag.

"Spear," he snarled.

Across the square, Sam saw Vamir standing on the walkway in front of the bookshop, looking perfectly serene. He raised an eyebrow and nodded to Sam.

Ugh, she thought as she stepped through the main gates. The pegasus snorted at her, but she ignored it and headed to the left-hand walkway. "Hw cm oo smf kt?" she muttered as she approached the elf.

He shrugged. "We have more control over our senses than you humans. Although I'll never understand why your kind find pegasi to be 'magical.'"

"Mm dmf!" Sam cried through the cloth. "Mm trmfh to tl—ggggh," she said, taking a deep breath and pulling the rag from her face. "I tried to tell them—these things are giant flying rats!"

"They travel in flocks, you know."

"I know!" Sam clamped the rag over her face and inhaled the relatively less noxious fumes of alcohol before removing it again. "Can we not go inside your shop?"

"Oh, of course," the elf said, gesturing for Sam to precede him.

Inside, Sam removed the rag and stuffed it into one pocket, breathing deeply of the musty, old-paper smell of the shop. "Gods defend the guilty," she sighed. "I don't understand how they haven't been hunted to extinction."

"They breed quite prolifically," Vamir pointed out.

"Oh, don't I know."

"You've encountered them before, then?" The elf managed to look amused.

Easy enough if you can shut your nose off, I guess. "Yeah, down south. Kahnsohocen. Whole group of them landed right in the middle of a battlefield, if you please. Acted as if nothing was happening, just started grazing and crapping everywhere."

The elf's eyes sparkled with humor. "I imagine that would have put a bit of a damper on the battle."

Sam snorted. "Shut it down completely. Mercs on both sides, and we agreed to just call it off. Forced our employers to play a game of chess to decide the outcome. Lost a hundred gold pieces, mind you, but we were desperate to get out."

Vamir chuckled quietly. "Well, if this one hasn't been joined by now, then it's probably an outcast. I imagine it'll move on soon enough. There's not that much forage here for it."

"You'd better hope so," Sam said darkly.

"I wanted to ask about the book," the elf said. *Way of the Divided Star.* Have you had a chance to read it?"

Oh, we're doing this, Sam thought, suddenly alert. "I have," she said slowly. "Some of it more than once."

"And?"

She nodded. "It's interesting. I mean. . . I definitely felt that way with Leeta, before she. . . before our last fight. We were exactly like what the book describes. One soul, inhabiting two bodies." A crushing wave of grief suddenly bore down on Sam's shoulders. "I miss her."

"And you've not felt that way. . . since?" The elf peered into her eyes.

"I. . ." *You did, didn't you? Just today.* "Maybe."

Vamir nodded knowingly. "Anything you can talk about?"

"No. Not. . . I don't think so."

"Fair enough."

"You think it has something to do with me fitting in. Here, I mean."

He shook his head. "I do not. The pub choosing you is more than sufficient evidence that you fit."

Sam tilted her head. "Then what?"

The old elf sighed and looked out the shop window. "There's

more than just fitting in, Sam. There's. . . happiness, if you dare. Destiny, even."

"Not a fan."

"Says the woman whose pub tells her the destinies of her customers."

"I try not to think about it."

He chuckled. "Again, fair enough. Could I just ask you a favor, then?"

"What's that?" Sam asked warily.

"Keep an open mind."

Sam stared at the old elf for a long moment. "Sure."

"Thank you."

They held each others' gaze for a few minutes. "I have to go back outside now, don't I?"

"You don't *have* to," Vamir countered with a grin. "I have a lot of books. We could read some."

"I met Knodalon."

Vamir raised an eyebrow. "Oh?"

"Says he used to hunt pegasi."

"Hardly surprising. I get the impression he's been around."

"With spears."

The elf shrugged. "I'd think arrows would just enrage them."

Sam nodded slowly and looked out the shop window. "Got a spear?"

———

Rag over her mouth and nose, Sam made her way around the walkway to the bakery. Notably, shop doors that would normally be thrown wide open at this time of day were closed up tight. "Hey, Makosi," she said as she slammed the bakery door shut behind her.

"Sam," the Fellis said. Her tail was slashing the air in frustration. "I don't suppose someone's worked out a solution?"

"To the flying horse?"

"That one, yes."

"No. Keep mucking out the village green, I guess."

"We've sent Kane and Sora out to help. The kids are taking it in turns, now."

"You all have a pretty keen sense of smell, no?"

"Not as strong as ogres, but yes. It isn't pleasant."

"Any chance of a sweet for a poor bartender who has to walk home through the fumes?"

Makota hissed softly in amusement and scooped two large pastries into a bag. "Cheese tart and a cloud. It's from this morning, but it'll still be wonderful. Just maybe. . ."

"Wait until I'm in the pub to eat it?"

"Certainly don't try outside," the baker said with a shudder. "You know, this is the first one I've seen."

"Pegasus? Sorry you had to see one at all."

"Me too."

Sam once again covered her mouth and nose and stepped out onto the walkway, quickly closing the bakery door behind her. She paused as Ivy, Cole's youngest, edged out into the green carrying a shovel and a bucket. The pegasus had spotted her and gone into a stiff, alert stance, its wings half-spread. It pawed the ground and snorted. "Ivy!" Sam called. The girl turned, and Sam sighed inside as she saw the delight in the girl's expression. *Little kids love flying horses, for some reason.* "Keep to the grass it's already chewed down! And watch your step! It only craps where it's already eaten!"

Ivy's eyes went wide, and she nodded quickly. As soon as she maneuvered onto an area of short-cropped grass—already going yellow—the pegasus snorted one last time, retracted its wings, and went back to its grazing. As Sam watched, its tail lifted and another stream of green-brown slime *plopped* from its behind.

Someone around here has to have a spear.

Cole and his family had constructed a pile of crates in the alley that led to their little farm—and to the Broken Claw's back door. Sam sighed and edged her way back to the main gate instead. The alcohol in her face cloth was running out, and she moved quickly to get to clear air before it vanished completely.

"You want to kill it, don't you?" The constable's voice greeted her as she edged past the main gates.

"Not specifically," Sam said, removing the rag from her mouth. "But I wouldn't be sad if someone did."

"Come in peace, stay in peace—"

"It's the *leave in peace* I'm hoping it'll get to," Sam countered with a grin.

"The kids love it."

"The kids aren't tired of cleaning up after it, yet."

"You really dislike them, don't you?"

Sam sighed. "As much as you'd dislike rats or any other kind of vermin. That's all they are. Someone just decided they're *pretty* vermin, and little children seem to fall in love with them. Where I've been, I've seen them overrun entire farms. Gnaw crops down to the ground and leave a trail of toxic waste behind them. And they're vicious."

Jen smiled and nodded. "But territorial?"

"Extremely. You saw this one snorting at Ivy just because she'd walked on an increasingly rare patch of unfouled, uneaten grass."

"Could we turn that to our advantage?"

Sam's eyes widened as her jaw dropped. "You want to. . . *use* that thing?" Jen shrugged, but her smile remained. "For *what*, pray the gods?"

"The village welcomes all."

"Not vermin, we don't. The store house explicitly excludes them."

The constable chuckled. "Fair enough. But vicious and territorial. . . is there a way we could turn that to our advantage?"

Sam shook her head. "I don't see—"

"It's only the one."

Now Sam stepped forward, leaning close to Jen. The constable took an involuntary step backward, but Sam quickly closed the distance again. "There's *never*," Sam said in a low, hot voice, "*only the one.*"

"Look!"

The two women separated at that cry. It had come from one of the day's last traders, who even now was pointing into the sky.

"Never only one," Sam repeated grimly.

eleven

. . .

SAM AWOKE SLOWLY the following morning, stretching and feeling little desire to open the pub. *Warm. Safe. Home.* She grinned. *Not busy.* After washing up and dressing, she thunked her way down the narrow staircase and through into the inn. Minnie was there, stirring a small pot of porridge. "Morning, Minnie," Sam said cheerfully.

"Morning, Sam. Not feeling like we'll have anyone in today, so I'm not putting on a stew. Or a big breakfast, for that matter, although if you'd like a bowl of porridge there'll be plenty."

Sam's stomach grumbled gently. "Actually, I think I'll go see what Makota's making."

"On quiet days she sometimes makes. . . oh, I forget the actual name. Something Fellis. They look like little neat little stacks of leaves, all paper-thin layers. She fills them with a soft, citrusy sweet cheese of some kind. They take forever to make even a small batch, but oh my goodness, are they wonderful."

"I am *so* in. Want me to bring you one if she made them?"

"Absolutely not, Sam," Minnie replied with a grin. "I'll be needing two, and Trevor can have one as well."

Sam smiled as pushed her way out the back door.

Her smile faded instantly as, rather than a slight sweet note in the air, all she could smell was pegasus. "Morning, Cole," she called. His entire tribe was weeding, tying up vines, picking ripe vegetables, and otherwise tending to the little farm.

"Morning, Sam," he called. "Makota has her danties in the oven."

"Minnie was just telling me about them, and I can't wait. Shame the flying horses won't leave."

Cole groaned. "Even Ivy's getting over them, aren't you?"

"Why do they have to be so *stinky?*" the little girl complained. "And when'll they leave?"

"Probably when we finally get tired of it and chase them out," Sam said, shaking her head sadly. "Think Minnie will mind if I use the back door?"

"Not at all," Cole said.

Another thin passageway separated the main building of the village from the little storehouse that served the garden, ending right at the bakery's back door. This was propped open, and now Sam could pick up the delicate, sweet scent of whatever Makota was making.

"Morning!" Sam called as she stepped in. The aromas were wonderfully stronger here, and as Minnie has promised they combined a light sugary note with the promise of bright citrus. The village farm featured only a few fruit trees, but one that Cole was especially proud of produced firm, round, red fruits that had a light, tart flavor. With care and the village's magic, these fruited almost year-round, going dormant for just a few sennights in the deepest part of winter.

"Morning!" Makota called. "Sam, is that you?"

"In the flesh and with the watering mouth."

"Hah!" the baker hissed. "They'll be out in a moment, but come have some tea with us."

Sam stepped through into the shop's front room, where the door was closed tightly—presumably against the smell of the pegasi who'd decided to make the village green their home. It had been two days since the second one had landed, and it seemed to Sam that the village's magic was the only reason the two hungry beasts hadn't eaten the green down to bare earth by now. "Who's on mucking duty today?"

"Darby again, poor boy," Masaaki said. "Especially with nobody expecting traders or travelers through today. Although the little scamp has been charging a copper to 'let' people see the creatures."

"Feels like this is one time the village's magic is working against us," Sam pointed out.

"With the grass?" Makota said, nodding. "We noticed that when the second one landed. I guess they get the same support we all do." She rose and headed past Sam into the back. "Those should be ready by now. Out in a moment!"

The pastries were *delightful*. Makota insisted Sam try one on the spot—meeting very little resistance, of course—as well as wrapping a few for her daughter to run over to Minnie and Trevor. The layers of pastry seemed impossibly thin, and the way they were stacked gave a soft, fluffy crunch as you bit in. The interiors were indeed filled with a soft, creamy cheese that had been flavored with the red citrus fruits. "These are heavenly," Sam said as she finished her first.

"They're my favorite," Makota said with a pleased expression. "But they take *candlemarks* to make, so I only bother once or twice a year, and only on days when it doesn't feel like we'll have any custom."

"Nothing at all today, then?"

"Definitely not," she said, shaking her head firmly. "We'll do a batch of brown bread just to replenish since it keeps so well, but otherwise we'll spend the day cleaning up a bit. It's been so busy the past few days I feel the place is a mess." Sam glanced around the shop and couldn't see so much as a speck of errant flour. "And then I think this afternoon I may just lounge about and read. Vamir found a new book I'm looking forward to reading." She frowned. "Although normally I'd enjoy it out in the green on the grass. I supposed I'll sit on the jetty instead."

"Cookbook?"

"I never mix work with pleasure," she said, grinning and twitching her whiskers. "No, it's a silly romance."

"You know, I'm due a new book as well. I think I'll pop over and see if Vamir's about."

"He will be. Just push on in, I imagine he'll have his door shut tight as well. Oh, and here," she added, quickly wrapping another warm confection in paper. "He loves these as much as anyone."

"Happy to be of service," Sam grinned, accepting the package. "Although I'm afraid there's a delivery fee." Makota laughed as she wrapped a second one and handed it over. "See you all later."

"Just hold your breath," Masaaki warned.

Sam sighed and pushed her way onto the front walkway. The smell of pegasi washed over her at once, and she quickly closed the door behind her. Darby was already out with his shovel and bucket, trying to stay out of the two beasts' way. Sam heard him sigh as one of them dropped another smeary load of dung before lowering its head and resuming its grazing. "Disgusting," Sam muttered. She held the pastries close to her nose as she hurried around to the bookshop. "Vamir?" she called as she stepped into the shop and closed the door behind her.

"Back here, Sam," the old elf's voice called from somewhere in the shop's depths.

Sam had spent only a few minutes at a time in the shop, and all of that had been in the front, so she was a little surprised to find a small area at the back that was actually open, rather than being packed tightly with tall, overstuffed shelves. Vamir was sitting at a small table, reading a book by oil lamp. He smiled as Sam approached. "Do I smell some of Makota's wonderful little leaf-stacks?"

"You do indeed," Sam said, setting one on the table. "Mind if I join you?"

"Please," he said, gesturing to a second chair as he unwrapped the pastry. "Oh, these are so delightful."

"Turned your nose back on, then?"

"For these, I'll risk even that creature's stench," he grinned.

They munched in companionable silence for a few moments. As she licked that last delicate, buttery crumbs from her fingers, Sam asked, "You know, if you don't mind, I'd love to know a bit more about where you're from. I've only ever met plains elves before."

"Well, we forest elves *are* particularly aloof and mysterious," he said with a grin, his almond-shaped eyes narrowing with good humor. "I'm from far, far to the east of here—from over the Skyreach Range, in fact. A region called the Darkestore Forest, abutting the Salten Sea."

Sam's eyebrows rose. "That's. . . wow. I've never been that far."

"I doubt anyone on this side of the Skyreach has."

"So what's life like in the Darkestore Forest?"

Vamir sighed and leaned back. "Beautiful, but difficult. Dangerous. That part of the world was home to some pretty serious battles, back in the day. Centuries ago. But they were liberal with their use of battle magics, and it. . . changed the lands, there. My people took up the task of cleaning it, once the powers involved finally managed to wipe themselves out. Whole new species of flora and fauna had been created. All beautiful, many deadly. We've been cleansing the. . . *difficult* magics ever since."

"So. . . you're a wizard?" Sam asked with a small frown.

"Me? Gods no," the old elf snorted. "I was a scout. Furthest thing possible from a. . . well, we call them mages. No, not a drop of magic in me, which is why I was a scout."

"I don't follow."

"The magical creatures out there, even those ones made *from* magic who don't actually *wield* magic, can all *sense* magic. From quite a ways off, actually. Some are drawn to it, others are repelled by it, but regardless, if you have any magic in you what-soever you're like a bright torch held in the night. Scouts are tasked with finding creatures, mainly the dangerous ones, and then calling others to deal with them."

"What's 'dealing with them' involve?"

"*Most* of the time," Vamir mused, chewing on the last bit of his pastry, "the mages can remove their magic. Tamp it down, so they can live as ordinary creatures. It's not uncommon for them to sterilize them in some cases, especially for the ones that breed prolifically. There's a variant of rabbit, for example, that can, if left unchecked, produce a litter every sennight. The battle-mages created them to overrun enemy positions—they've wickedly sharp teeth and a taste for blood. But they'll eat anything that can, and left alone they'll eat everything in sight. There are only a couple of active colonies at this point, but we'd never managed to stop them completely. Only takes two for them to start over."

"Wow."

"And *sometimes*," he continued, a sad look coming across his face, "we would regrettably have to kill. Mainly for the largest, most dangerous beasts—basilisks, colddrakes, wyrven. Rare beasts all, and for the most part happy to keep to themselves. But if they happened across even a pocket of civilization, their battle instincts would kick in and nothing short of death would stop them from killing everything they could sense."

"Ugh."

"Indeed. But it's why I tend to be gently inclined toward the non-inimical ones."

Ah. "Like the pegasi."

He nodded. "Like the pegasi. Although as far as I know, those are natural creatures, not made from magic."

Sam cocked an eyebrow. "Seriously? They seem really badly designed. And somehow I think they defecate more than they actually ingest."

"I've observed them before. They *are* somewhat poorly designed, especially in the musculature that controls their wings.

They're actually incredibly awkward in the air—terrible turning radius, and if they tried to swoop like a hawk I think their wings would snap off. That's how you can tell, though. If they'd been created, I suspect they'd be better designed. As for the. . . defecating," he said with a shrug, "I think they just have really inefficient digestive systems. They don't chew their cud like proper horses. No, they seem like some sort of natural crossbreed, to me."

"They're still disgusting."

He laughed. "Objectively true. Do you think we'll have to run them out?"

"Sooner or later," Sam grimaced. "Smallest herd—flock, whatever—I've ever seen was a dozen." Vamir's eyes widened. "Yeah, exactly. But they're hard to run off. Very, very territorial."

"Well. I wish I could do more to help." He tilted his head. "Actually, I might. This is feeling like it's becoming a real need, no?"

Sam's brow wrinkled. "I don't understand."

The elf smiled. "My shop's gift. If this is a real need. . . perhaps I'll find a book on the subject."

Comprehension dawned. "Oh. Oh, yes. That'd be *very* helpful. And trust me, there's a *very real* need."

"I shall begin looking at once," he said, standing up. Sam followed him to the front of the shop, where, through the window, she could see the constable staring at the pegasi.

"I think I'll go talk to Jen," Sam sighed. "Let me know if you find anything."

"Assuredly."

"Ready to plot their demise, yet?" Sam asked as she closed the bookshop door behind her.

Jen sighed. "It's not sustainable, you're right about that. If only they didn't make such a. . . mess."

"There'll be more," Sam cautioned her. "What's Warren doing?"

The blacksmith was walking slowly into the village green,

and his son had already moved off to the covered walkway on the opposite side. The ogre was taking very small, very deliberate steps, with his eyes tracking the two glossy black pegasi. In one hand was a heavy leather halter, and Sam could see a second one swinging from his hip.

"He might be taking matters into his own hands," Jen murmured.

"He's going to get himself killed. Or badly maimed," Sam warned.

"He won't get violent," Jen disagreed.

"*He* won't," Sam countered.

Already, the pegasi had stopped grazing and were eying Warren. The new arrival—a female, this time—was stepping skittishly, turning to keep Warren in her sight. Her wings were fluttering nervously. The stallion took a couple of quick steps toward the smith, snorting in irritation and rippling his own wings.

Warren took another step, his empty hand outstretched.

The stallion raised both front hooves from the ground, spreading his wings slightly for balance, and then brought those hooves down hard on the grass. He whickered a warning.

"Warren," Jen called calmly. "What's the plan, here?"

"I was thinking maybe we'd be happier with them in the stable yard," he said easily, taking another small step toward the stallion. The mare backed away, mantling her wings nervously as the stallion shook his head and snorted again.

"There's not much grass in that yard," Sam pointed out.

"There's hay."

"They can *fly*, you know," Sam added. "Down south there are people who tame the damn things and actually ride them."

Warren frowned. "I'm pretty heavy, and with a halter on its head. . ."

The stallion seemed to have a pretty good notion of Warren's plan as well, and clearly wasn't intending to cooperate. This time, he reared up fully, front hooves slicing at the air as he neighed a warning, his wings spreading to full extension before snapping back to his flanks.

Warren took another cautious step forward, his attention now fully on the male pegasus.

"Warren," Sam called softly, realizing what was happening. "It's the fem—"

The mare lunged at Warren. Caught completely off-guard, he barely managed to dodge her snapping teeth, and as her wings flicked outwards to balance her, she reared up on her hind legs and lashed out with her front, mimicking the move the stallion had just made—but with far more lethal intent. Warren dove for the ground, rolling back toward the main gate as the mare neighed her anger.

"Dad!" Darby screamed.

"Stay!" the constable ordered the boy as she stepped to the edge of the walkway. She'd stiffened her right arm and was preparing to step down to the grass.

"No!" Sam hollered, grabbing Jen's left forearm. The other woman made to pull away, but Warren was already rolling out of reach. The mare flapped her wings once, snorting loudly, and then stepped back behind the stallion. "She's good now," Sam said loudly. "Warren! Just stay low and back out!"

The mare was still gnashing her teeth, but the stallion stepped between her and the ogre, one wing spread protectively over the mare. Warren was scurrying backwards, one hand brushing the grass for balance until he was between the gate turrets.

"They're still prey animals, not predators," Sam said, still loud enough for Warren to hear. "They won't attack, but they don't like being touched."

"You said people. . . tamed them," Jen said softly.

"Crazy people," Sam said in a quieter voice. "Yeah."

"How?"

"Long ropes with lassos," Sam replied promptly. "You have

to get three or four around their heads at once, though. They. . . it's a bit of a show, honestly. They have competitions."

"Hmm." The constable stared at the pegasi for a bit longer. The mare let out another annoyed snort before she folded her wings and went back to grazing. "Leave the dung for a bit, Darby," she called. "Let them settle." Then, with another hard look at the flying horses, she stepped off the walkway and stalked out the main gate.

"Bit of excitement this morning, eh?"

Sam turned to her right and saw Leota sitting on a bench in front of her home. "Yeah, a bit." She could see Warren walking back to his smithy. "At least nobody got hurt." She turned and stepped closer to the witch. Instantly, the smell of the pegasi faded.

Leota caught her expression and grinned. "A little indulgence. The weather's so nice, and you know I don't get out much."

"Why is that?"

She tilted her head a bit, considering. "You know, you and I haven't had much of a chance to chat. It seems like it'll be a slow day. Fancy a tea?"

Sam smiled. "You know, that'd be just the thing. I—" Her eyes flew open as the pub *summoned* her. "I may need a rain check," she said quickly, turning to go. "Sorry!" The pub's need *pulsed* at her, and she broke into a run.

"Tell everyone something's coming!"

twelve

. . .

WARREN WAS ALREADY STANDING in the middle of the trade road as ten men on horseback clopped to a halt just inside the gate. Sam hurried toward him, and glanced back to see Jen hot on her tail. As they neared the group, Sam's stomach clenched as she recognized the four thugs from the other day.

"We laid down the rules last time," the constable called in a stern voice. "And they stand. Come in peace, stay in peace, leave in—"

"My men informed me of your 'rules,'" the lead horseman sneered.

Sam quickly assessed the group. The four thugs were the least-proficient looking ones of the lot. The one in front looked like more of a leader—he sat straighter in this saddle, his clothes were of a far better cut, and his horse seemed far better trained. The four who'd been here before weren't wearing their heavy leather jackets, and as Sam scanned them all, she couldn't see any sign of the inscribed metal badges. *Maybe the village's magic will be able to work, this time,* she thought hopefully.

"But we bring no violence," the leader continued as his men began grinning. "Indeed, we bring beneficent news! No more will you have to fear the predations of bandits and thieves! No more will you labor to maintain this beautiful, essential trade road for free! No more will you suffer the irregular hordes and crowds that must surely descend on your. . . *fair village* in weather so mild as this!"

"What are you talking about?" Sam asked.

"Why, fair lady,"—he paused as one of the four thugs muttered something Sam didn't catch—"good barkeep, we mean to establish a toll here in your pleasant village!"

Several other villagers had stepped into the road to see what has happening. Minnie was standing on the walkway in front of her inn, Susan was standing in the smithy's entrance, and Pavati was standing in front of the fishmonger's shop. All wore concerned expressions.

"A toll," Jen said flatly.

"A simple concept, but one possibly unknown to you in these distant parts," the leader said, his twisted grin belying the prettiness of his words. "We simply—"

"You charge people to ride through the village. We know what a toll is," Sam said, shaking her head in disgust. "No thanks."

"And you speak for the entire population of. . . whatever this place is called?" the man probed, his grin not faltering in the slightest.

"I do," the constable said cooly. "And it's a 'thanks, but no thanks.' We're doing just fine the way we are."

More muttering from the thugs. "Ah," the man said, slipping down from his saddle and striding confidently toward Sam and Jen. "My men tell me you're the local strong-arm."

"Constable," Jen corrected.

"Constable," he said, nodding politely. "Allow me to introduce myself. I am Ellis Manfred, leader of this small troupe of adventurers."

"Adventurers," Jen said.

"Of course, of course!" Ellis gushed, his twisted grin still firmly in place. Several of his men were chuckling. "Why, we've been freeing small villages such as this one of the burdens of defending themselves for years, now."

"I'll bet," Sam muttered.

"But we've decided to settle down. To put down roots, as it were! And when my men encountered this lovely village, populated by such friendly people but clearly lacking anything in the way of formal defenses, well." He placed a hand on his chest. "Our hearts broke for you. And so we hastened here. Of course, we intend to place no additional burden on you!"

"Oh?" Jen asked, her voice still cool.

"Never!" Ellis cried, his grin widening. "You see, all of our services shall be funded solely through the collection of tolls on those passing through. More than enough to sustain us. Although, of course, we will have to come to some arrangements regarding our housing and upkeep."

"Upkeep," Jen said.

"Meals, beverages, that kind of thing," Ellis said easily, waving a hand in the air. "Perfectly standard terms, of course."

"Oh, of course," Jen said, nodding. "I understand completely."

"You do?" Ellis seemed a bit put off by that.

"Oh, absolutely. We house you and feed you, we give you our ale, and you charge money for everyone who passes through to do business with us. Money that you keep, of course. Because it's a toll. And we get. . . let me guess, your protection."

Ellis' grin struggled a bit under Jen's biting sarcasm. "Exactly so. 'Round the clock security, in fact."

"No thanks," Jen said flatly. "You can go, now."

"Oh, I think not," Ellis said in a dangerous, low voice. His grin had returned full force. "And in point of fact, I believe we'll see to those accommodations straight away. Boys?"

His men slid out of their saddles almost as one, and Sam was reluctantly impressed at how well-behaved the horses were. Each of them simply stood in place, showing no inclination to wander off and start grazing. With Ellis in the lead, the ten of them pushed past Sam and Jen, making for the village's main gate.

Sam reached for Nailbiter's hilt, but Jen laid a gentle hand on her forearm, giving a soft shake of her head. She fell in behind the men and Sam moved quickly to keep up, hearing Warren's heavy footsteps just behind her.

"Decent fortifications, in fact," Ellis observed as he walked. "Solid stone. Why, this place is all but a fortress! We'll be able to get tolls set up quite easily, I think." He *tskd* a bit as his eyes tracked down and saw the debris piled up against the gates. "We'll get you to do something about these, of course. No point having gates if you don't—oh."

He'd looked up and spotted the pegasi grazing in the square. The mare looked up curiously, snorted lightly, and went back to tearing up grass. "You have a. . . zoo?"

"They live here," Sam said. "Although you know, if you really want to earn your pay, you can get them to leave."

Ellis turned to her, his nose wrinkling. "They *reek.*"

"Yeah, we noticed."

"Simon, Allard, get the horses," Ellis ordered. Two of his men —none of them the four thugs from before—nodded and began walking into the green.

"They're pegasi," Sam noted.

"They're vermin," Ellis countered.

Sam shrugged. "You've got me there."

Ellis stepped forward, his eyes raking across the arc of shop doors. "How many of these are currently uninhabited?" he asked. "Some of my men can happily live two to a room, especially once we have our shifts established, but—" his eyes snapped to his men as the pegasi screeched, both mare and stallion spreading their wings and rearing. "Quick about it, men!" he ordered.

"I don't think they want to go, Ellis," one of the men— Symon, Jen thought—said warily.

"They're extremely territorial," Jen said easily. "Why, given our total lack of defenses and strength, we've just been ever so at odds about what to even do about them. Even our tame ogre can't get near them."

Sam smothered a smirk as Warren obligingly hollered, "Pretty flying horses hurt ogre!"

The pegasi were either very lucky or were actually. . . *smart,* Sam thought. They'd separated, this time, the mare sidling to the left while the stallion pranced right, putting the two men in between them. Spreading their wings—they really *did* have an incredible wingspan—they began short-stepping forward, boxing the two men in.

"Boss!" the other man—Allard—called, his tone showing some well-earned panic.

"Call them off," Ellis growled, turning to Jen.

The constable shrugged. "They're not pets. We've no control over them. Literally, we want them gone more than you do."

The stallion reared again, his front hooves lashing out for the men's heads. Both of them crouched low and managed to scramble out from between the enraged pegasi, backing toward the main gate.

The pegasi snorted in unison and moved away from the gate, their wings still half-extended.

"Boss, we're going to need ropes. Halters. Maybe nets," Symon panted as he and Allard rejoined the group. "Those things are—"

"What's all this noise?"

Everyone turned to see Leota strolling through the grass, just along the walkway in front of the tea shop and herbalist's, toward the main gate. The pegasi snorted and moved well clear of her, shuffling toward the grocer's side of the grassy square.

"Who's this, the village crone?"

Sam frowned. Leota wasn't even *old,* although she did have a frailness about her.

"I'm the village witch," Leota said, stopping between the gate turrets and crossing her arms. "Who're you?"

"Kill the witch," Ellis ordered.

With a *hiss* of steel against leather, one of his men—an impossibly tall, lithe man with the build and grace of a swordfighter, drew a thin, whiplike blade and stepped toward the village gates. In almost the same moment, there was a *snick*, followed by a rattling sound as half the man's blade clattered on the dirt road. Ellis turned his head quickly enough to see the bladeless hilt of Sam's weapon settling back onto its belt hanger.

His eyes rose slowly to meet hers. "That's a Changeling weapon."

She nodded. "It is."

"So *you're* the witch," he growled, turning toward her.

"No," Leota said firmly, *"I'm* still the witch. She's a former merc who has earned her place here." Ellis turned back to Leota. "And right now, I'm very much the one you should be worried about. I'll ask again, what is the *meaning* of all this?"

"These gentlemen are planning to set a toll on the village," Jen called. "To pay for their services in defending us. In addition to room and board, of course."

"Ah," Leota said, nodding slowly. "Well, much as we appreciate the offer, I'm afraid the answer is no."

"Witch," Ellis snarled, raising a hand to motion one of his men.

"I wouldn't," Leota snapped, freezing the man in place with a look. "Stop blustering for a moment, whoever you are, and *feel* where you are. The village can feel you. I know you can feel it." Everyone was silent for a moment. Sam looked sidelong at one of the thugs, and saw confusion settle on his expression. "Ah," the witch continued, "you're sensing it now. Come in peace. Stay in peace. Leave in peace. It's not just a slogan. It's the reason this place *exists.*" Her eyes moved from one bandit's to the next's. "And there's more. *We serve all.* All who follow the rules of peace are welcome, and they'll receive sustenance, shelter, and whatever assistance we can offer. You can't change that." Again, her eyes darted quickly between the intruders'. "No tolls."

Another *hiss* of a sword being drawn was met with another *snick,* and this time three-quarters of a blade thumped to the road before Sam replaced her weapon at her hip.

"Well, I'd say that violates the peace clause," Leota said with a firm nod. "I'll offer you one more bit of advice, whomever you all are."

"And what's that?" Ellis said nastily, reaching for his own weapon.

"Go *far.* I've frankly never tested this and I don't know how far beyond the trade road gates it'll reach."

Ellis looked behind him, gauging his men's readiness, and that was the only reason Sam saw the change come over his face. Confusion first, followed by a clenched jaw that was accompanied by a *very* audible roiling in his guts—and the guts of his men. Then a stark, sudden realization, followed by a pale discomfort.

He turned back to Leota.

She shrugged. "I'd run."

Warren was already running back to the men's horses, hollering at the top of his formidable lungs. Well-trained or not, few horses cared to stand their ground in the face of a charging, bellowing ogre. All ten of them turned and fled, galloping as fast as their hooves could carry them out the gate and down the trade road.

Ellis and his men followed as quickly as they could, waddling in an awkward half-walk, half-run as they fought to contain whatever they'd eaten so far that day. One of the men didn't make it, collapsing to the road and groaning in misery. One of his companions stopped for him, wrinkling his nose in disgust but nonetheless helping the man to his feet. The two of them leaned on each other as the man who'd fallen continued to moan and walk. . . oddly.

His leather breeches were suspiciously dark around his backside.

The rest of the villagers turned out to watch them men hobble out of town.

"You okay?" Jen asked softly, walking quickly to Leota's side. The witch remained standing, but she seemed to lean into Jen for support.

"I will be. Directing it like that is. . . challenging." She frowned. "And I don't think it'll stick."

"You can't—"

"You know the village needs more," Leota said urgently. The other villagers turned away as if this didn't concern them, raising their voices and wondering if the men would make it to a nice, quiet bush before everything gave loose.

Sam remained focused on the constable and the witch, stepping closer. "Two anchors," Jen murmured.

"And also the icosagon," Leota said tightly, leaning more heavily on Jen's arm. "Help me back to my home. Galhani," she called out more loudly, "any chance for one of your restorative teas?"

"Coming right up, my dear," the gnome said, rushing back toward her shop.

Everyone was splitting up now, heading back to their individual or family concerns. Sam remained in the trade road, just outside the main gates. She stared at the pegasi, who'd warily gone back to grazing. The stallion looked up, met her eyes, and lifted his tail to drop another slimy load of excrement behind him.

What, Sam thought, *in the four hells is an icosagon?*

"Sam!" Sam started. Leota was standing on the walkway just outside the tea shop, leaning even more heavily on Jen's arm. "We need to talk."

No kidding, lady, Sam thought grimly, trudging toward the witch's home.

thirteen

. . .

SAM WAITED PATIENTLY until Leota had settled herself on the bench in front of her home, Galhani had arranged a pot of fresh-smelling tea and a plate of light-colored cheese slices, and Jen had finally stalked away.

"Good job, out there," Jen said quietly as she passed.

"Sam," Leota said as Sam walked up. "Please, have a seat." Someone had pulled a chair over from the tea shop, and Sam sank into it.

Whatever magic Leota had cast to block the pegasi smell was back, and. . . Sam frowned. The village children obviously hadn't been playing on the green like they'd used to, but the village still made *noise*. It was eerily quiet.

Leota smiled as she noted Sam's expression. "Gives us a bit of privacy while we speak. Not that anyone hasn't heard my story, but. . . I guess I've learned to be cautious."

"Your story?" Sam asked.

"Mmm. Please help yourself to some tea. And the cheese is wonderful—it's a very mild flavor, which I prefer, but the ladies age it in some kind of ash coating, which gives it a really lovely character."

"Oh." Sam poured herself a cup of tea and settled back to

listen. The tea *was* refreshing—light and airy, with just a touch of mint and something floral.

"Mind, I'd love to hear *your* story first, if you don't mind."

Sam grinned. "Nate didn't tell you?"

Leota smiled back. "Of course he did. But it's not the same."

"It's probably not all that interesting. Grew up in a poor family, only child. We all worked hard, and I was a bit of a tomboy. Had an old fighter in the village and he started teaching me sword, using a couple of sticks. I got good at it, he said. I was just passing seventeen when a merc troop was passing through our village. Saw me practicing with old Reuger and offered to train me up proper, give me a spot, in exchange for a five-year contract."

"Which I assume you took?"

"Four hells, yes. My parents practically signed the contract for me—best chance for getting out and making something for myself."

Leota tilted her head. *"For* yourself? Not *of* yourself?"

Sam chuckled. "Ma was very specific on that point. Said, 'Samantha, you don't need to prove anything to anyone, but you do need to earn what you want and need from this world. Go off and find out what that is, and then get it, and don't let anyone stand in your way.'"

"Very wise."

"They both were."

"They're. . ." Leota began delicately.

"Passed, long since," Sam said, smiling softly. "Lived to a proper old age, and I sent back what I could to help make them comfortable."

Leota murmured something comforting and asked, "And so you lived the merc life?"

"Switched companies here and there," Sam nodded. "As you do. Figured I'd keep doing it until someone or something finally split me in half." She smiled ruefully and touched her forehead. "Until something almost did."

"Took the fight out of you?"

"In one breath. Decided I'd seen enough of this world and fought at least half of it. I didn't know what I wanted to do next, just that I didn't want *that* anymore."

"And you found your way here."

"On the road to nowhere. At least, I didn't have a destination in mind."

"That," Leota said, nodding to Sam's waist, "is an impressive souvenir. I assume you know how rare Changeling artifacts are?"

Sam's hand brushed Nailbiter's hilt. "I've come to. Took her off another woman. She was a bit older than me at the time." Sam's eyes lost focus as she thought back. "Amazing fighter. She just. . . stood out, on the field. Seemed like we were fighting our way to each other."

Leota frowned a bit. "And the sword just let you. . . *take* it?"

"Oh, no," Sam said, smiling faintly at the memory. "We fought for. . . well, probably three or four minutes, but it felt like candlemarks. Some of my company said, afterwards, that it was like the rest of the battle just made room around us."

"And you bested her."

Sam shook her head. "No, that's the funny thing about Changeling weapons. At some point. . . it's like it just *decided*. She, the other fighter, just gave me this kind of sad smile and the blade *vanished*. I was full into a swing, couldn't pull it at that point." Sam's gaze grew even more distant. "She went down with a smile."

Leota was nodding slowly. "It's said Changeling artifacts have a mind of their own."

Sam shrugged, coming back to the present. "I've never felt a *mind* so to speak. But definitely. . . it has a *will*. Out there, by the gate, that was as much the sword as me."

"Do you think you'll go the same way? In a fight, where the sword just. . . decides?"

Sam shrugged. "Could be. Funny thing is, I don't think it *likes* fighting. With me, at least, it's always been the shortest way to the end of the fight. Maybe it's ready to retire here as well."

"You seem to have a pretty open mind about. . . magic," Leota commented as Sam sipped her tea. "And you certainly haven't seemed bothered about the people here in the village."

"I've seen a lot," Sam said with a shrug. "Had a lot of companions. Magic doesn't bother me a bit, if that's what you mean. We had wizards in the last company I was with."

"Ah," Leota said with a slight nod, taking her own sip of tea. "So do you know the differences between a wizard and a witch?"

"Witches are women, wizards are men?"

Leota smiled. "True, although that's actually more of an *outcome* than a *requirement.*"

Sam's brow creased in puzzlement. "Not sure I understand that."

"Few do," Leota admitted. "There are actually two distinct kinds of magic in the world. At least two—there are actually theories that the elves' magic is a third type, and that the natural magic used by beasts—like those pegasi—is yet another type. But for humans, two types."

"I didn't know pegasi were actually magical."

"Horses couldn't possibly fly without magic, no matter how big their wings," Leota snorted delicately. "In fact, I'm pretty sure it's how they hide from the village."

"What do you mean, 'hide?'"

"They're literally invisible to it. I've tried more than a few times over the past couple of days to get them to leave, to coerce them, to make them feel fear, anything, but the village's magic doesn't even acknowledge they exist. Even blocking their smell requires me to block *all* smells."

"Ah." Which would be why the ever-present, cool scent of the lake had vanished as well.

Leota continued. "Anyway, for humans, the different types of magic plays into how we talk about managing magic. If you have the gift, it flows into you all the time, and it's up to you to do something with it. So we have this idea of channels, which exist in your mind, and we used those to collect, store, and direct magic as we need it. But you're born to handle only one type. High magic, or what some of us prefer to call active magic, is what wizards use. That gets you your battle magics, the major healing spells, enchanted weapons, that kind of thing."

"And that's men? Wizards, I mean?"

"As far as we know, only men are born with the channels to direct active magic, yes. When women get the gift, it's for common magic, and you become a witch. It's a much broader magic, actually, but it's less showy, more low-key."

"And that's what you got."

"Actually," Leota said slowly, "I was *born* Leonard and trained as a battle wizard."

Sam blinked several times as she sipped her tea. "You might have to help me out with that one."

Leota chuckled. "That is the calmest response I've ever gotten to that, so thank you. When I was thirteen, my gifts came to me all at once, as they often do with young wizards. I was sent off to school and trained for combat magics, as most wizards are. I eventually took a contract with a mercenary company not unlike your Vixens—Trond's Terrors, we called ourselves." She frowned a bit. "Our first big engagement was a battle down in Shorehaven, along the Amber Sea. They were getting a wave of invaders from one of the Bright Islands—amazing how well-equipped those islanders are—and Shorehaven has almost nothing in the way of standing defenses."

Her eyes grew distant. "Have you ever seen those ship-mounted siege weapons? They're horrific. They can launch balls of flaming pitch further than you'd think. Shorehaven is mostly timber and thatch—if just one of those things hit, that'd be the end of it.

"They had me construct a shield—a monstrous one. But you know what? It was easy. The big magics had always come easily to me, right from the outset. *Channels of brass,* they'd told me in school. And so I cast it, and it worked. I caught four, maybe five of those giant balls, and just let them slide right down into the sea.

"But then they started firing something else." Leota's expression grew troubled as she remembered. "Something imbued with magic—and those islanders aren't supposed to even *have* wizards. It. . . *stuck* to my shield and. . . it's hard to explain. *Thrummed.* My shield started to vibrate. The word doesn't convey how awful it was. It's like *I* was vibrating, like I was about to come apart at the seams.

"So I poured more magic in, started really sweating just holding it together.

"Then they fired another.

"Fortunately by then, someone had gotten a bead on their ships and started firing three of our large ballistas at them. Punched right through their hulls, and that distracted them pretty quickly. But. . . I couldn't stop the shield. Those two *things* were still stuck to it, and the magic just kept pouring out of me. I screamed. . . I remember screaming.

"But then I blacked out." She took a sip of tea and nibbled on a piece of cheese. Sam's eyes were wide, but she said nothing.

"They tell me I was unconscious for two months. Sedated, while my channels tried to heal. Magical damage is. . . tricky. When they finally brought me out of it I couldn't do the active magics anymore. I tried, and it just wouldn't come. But I could still *feel* magic. I started being able to do small things. Campfires, lights for reading, that kind of thing." She sighed. "Common magic. Not something a mercenary company really values. So I took my cashier and left."

"I don't. . ." Sam started slowly when Leota didn't continue.

"Magic *makes* us, when you've got the gift," she said. "My channels had been broken, and when they healed, they healed. . . *different.* Not wrong. But they healed as a witch's. And over the course of that next year. . . I *became* a witch. In every way that matters." Her eyes cleared, and she looked meaningfully at Sam. "I've started to wonder if I wasn't always meant to be this way."

Sam simply stared, fascinated. "What do you mean?"

"I don't know. It's hard to describe, even to myself. But ever since my magic came back, ever since it was different. . . I've felt more comfortable in my skin than I ever did. More settled. It's like, this is how I was *supposed* to be, and everything before was just. . . getting by."

"I think I understand."

"But I still have traces of wizardry in me. I gather a *lot* of magic. Too much to use up with common magic, and my channels never healed well enough to store much. So I *have* to do something with it."

"The. . . village?" Sam asked softly.

Leota nodded. "Before I found this place, I was. . . well, just call it what it is. *Dangerous.* If I wasn't casting minor spells almost constantly—and I mean waking up four times a night to light a fire or ward something or whatever—then magic would build up in me. I didn't have any safe way to release it in large batches—common magic doesn't have big, flashy, power-hungry spells. And my channels can't handle pushing a lot at once. And so once or twice. . . things went wrong."

"That doesn't sound good."

Leota grimaced. "It wasn't. One time someone in a pub had spiked my wine, and I didn't wake up all night. When I finally woke up, my purse was empty and the pub—and a dozen buildings around it—had been obliterated. The *people* were fine, but it's like the structured themselves just. . . went away. Nobody suspected me—who's ever heard of a frail woman like me wielding that kind of power? but I hoofed it out of there pretty quickly."

"And then you came here."

She nodded. "This place doesn't *need* a witch. Not like it needs the pub and the constable. But when it has one, it takes most of my magic. I'm left a little, for small tasks like blocking smells," she said with a grin, "and I can *direct* its magic more purposefully than it would on its own. With a witch in this house, the village is more aware, more alert. Without one, it's. . . sleepier. But directing it is difficult, and I'm frankly not a strong person. Not since Shorehaven. That trick with giving those men the runs took it out of me, and I'll be sitting down or in bed for most of a sennight."

"So was that *you* or the *village* that did that?"

"Mostly both. They were already making it testy—it reads intent, which is how half of our shops work, obviously, and it didn't like theirs. Normally, it'd let the constable handle it, but it doesn't seem to realize that with that many men, violence would be the only outcome. We're not going to *talk* them down. I kind of. . . called its attention to that. Suggested that maybe if they didn't *want* to be here, they'd go. Giving them the runs is something we could attribute to bad water, right? It tends to lean on things that have other, plausible explanations."

"But it won't stick."

The witch shook her head. "No. They'll be back, be sure of it."

"Because we're not complete."

Leota nodded slowly, her eyes on Sam's. "I believe so."

"You mentioned the pub and the constable," Sam said. "I heard you talking to Jen about them. She said. . . anchors? Like on a ship?"

Leota nodded and sighed again. "The village can function with only those two roles. Even the locations of the pub and the gaol are emblematic—they're on opposite ends of the trade road, just inside. So long as there's a constable and a barkeep, the village's magic works to some degree. It'll welcome peaceful travelers and provide them what it can."

"There was another word you used. Eye-coss something."

She nodded. "Icosagon, yes. That's where Jen and I have a bit of a disagreement. A moment." She stepped inside her house and returned a moment later carrying a rolled parchment, which she passed to Sam.

Sam unrolled it, but couldn't make any sense of the symbols written in heavy black ink.

"Pretty?" she said.

Leota chuckled. "It's ancient Mistral. The race this mountain range was named for, in fact."

"They were native to here?"

"To the entire *continent*, at one time. But then they started vanishing, and this mountain range was their last known population. Possibly the seat of their kingdom or whatever they had. Centuries and centuries ago. But the language is well-preserved —it's how wizards document their spells."

"Wait, so you can *read* this?"

The witch nodded. "I can. Well, I can approximate it. The Mistrals had some concepts that we don't. But what's interesting is that even though the village has had witches before, *it's never had one who was trained as a wizard.*"

Sam's eyes widened. "Nobody's ever been able to read this?"

"I doubt it."

"So what's it say?"

Leota's lips twitched with humor. "It translates as poetry. Just don't say I didn't warn you." She took the scroll back from Sam and began to recite:

> *Rooted deep where spirits soar,*
> *Echoes of history, tales galore.*
> *Embraced by strength, a sacred vow,*
> *In nature's cradle, we stand proud.*

Tomorrow's dawn, a beckoning call,
Destiny's dance, never to stall.
Here, solace reigns, fears take flight,
Within the fortress of twenty, bathed in light.

"Whoever wrote that would make a terrible bard," Sam grinned when she finished.

"If you heard me sing it, you'd say something far worse, trust me. But I believe it's meant to describe the village's. . . founding principle, maybe."

"That last line. . ."

Leota nodded. "Fortress of twenty, yes. The icosagon."

"What's the word mean?"

"It's a twenty-sided polygon. A single element with twenty faces. Difficult to carve, if you're into whittling—you have to be very precise. If you look around the village, there are carvings in the stone, here and there. Two-dimensional, of course, and most of them quite worn by weather, but I believe they're trying to depict one."

"Twenty-sided. . ."

"It's *us*. The shopkeepers. Warren, Prudence, the dryads—they count as one—you, Minnie, Cole, Galhani, Vamir, Tyran, Alred, Calder, Dardrad, Makota, Lucy, Jen, me, even Dexter."

"And Knodalon?"

"*Especially* Knodalon."

Sam ran through the names again. "But that's only eighteen."

"Which means we're missing two. Aside from the pub and the gaol, the village isn't picky about who opens a shop here. But I think it wants a full twenty to. . . be its full self."

"Has it ever had that?"

"Not that anyone remembers. Well. . . anyone but Knodalon. And he won't discuss it with me."

"He's been here. . . a while."

Leota snorted. "I'm pretty sure he's been here *forever*. I actually suspect he might be Mistral."

"You're kidding."

"I am not."

Sam sat quietly for a moment, sipping the last of her tea. Then she became aware of someone staring at her. She scanned the part of the village she could see and. . . "What is *her* deal?"

Leota followed Sam's gaze. "Prudence? Hmm. That's. . . a complicated story. You should ask her yourself."

"She's only ever given me the evil eye."

"That's not the evil eye," Leota retorted lightly. "I can show you a real one sometime. That's just mistrust. I got it, too. She's still uncomfortable around me, in fact. But. . . you should talk to her about it, when you get a chance."

"I guess." Then, after another long moment of silence, "So how do we get two more?"

Leota shrugged. "That's kind of your job. The pub will let you know when someone's meant to stay. But it means we can't be having those men set up tolls."

"Well, it's not like people have a way around us, toll or no."

"No, but. . . some traffic would stop coming. And if we were only getting people willing to pay a toll, or too desperate not to. . ."

Sam nodded. "Yeah, I see your point."

"So all we can do is—oh, bitter hells."

"Gods, not a third one," Sam sighed as another glossy black pegasus touched down and trotted off its momentum. Leota dropped her sound barrier and they could hear the other two whickering a welcome to their new kin.

"Sam," Leota said, her voice suddenly urgent as she leaned forward.

"I see it," Sam said grimly, rising quickly.

Prudence's little toddler had clambered off the walkway and was running toward the new arrival.

fourteen

. . .

EITHER NUMBERS HAD GIVEN the creatures more confidence, or they were particularly afraid of knee-high, stumbling bipeds with a tendency to drool. And squeal with glee, as Prudence's was.

"Bryant!" she screamed as she realized what was happening.

"Stay back!" Sam shouted. All around the walkway, shop doors were being flung open as shopkeepers and their families investigated the cries.

Sam's mind sank into an approximation of a battlefield: enemy positions, vectors, threat priorities. One of the pegasi had its head down toward Bryant and was pawing the ground as it huffed a warning. Its wings were half-spread for balance, and Sam could see the tension in its hindquarters.

The other two had wheeled to face their "attacker," wings similarly spread as they stepped backwards through their own dung to give the lead mare room to defend them.

Sam's brain did the math automatically, as she bolted toward the lead mare and, at the last possible moment, leapt into the air.

It probably weighed seventy stone to her twelve, but it was top-heavy and not designed to resist lateral force. It also, for some reason, wasn't paying attention to her. She tucked into a ball and slammed into its shoulder. It didn't go down, but it stumbled heavily to one side with a shriek. Sam's feet hit the ground, and she stayed in a half-crouch as she pulled Nailbiter from her belt. With a *snick*, its blade appeared, phantom reflections of blue and purple.

In her peripheral vision, she saw Cole dash over and snag Bryant, holding the boy under one arm as he retreated to the walkway and passed the toddler to his mother. Dimly, she heard Prudence sobbing with relief, but Sam was focused on the three angry horses in front of her.

They'd repositioned themselves with the stallion in front and the two mares back and to either side. *That's a standard move for them, then,* she thought, *which means it'll be one of the mares who lunges first.* "Now look," she said, panting a bit, "we'd much prefer to leave you in peace. Actually, we'd very much prefer if you'd *leave* in peace, but there's no—"

The mare on the left whinnied as she lunched forward. Less than an eye blink later, she'd screamed, scrambled backwards, and was flapping her wings in annoyance. A thin, bright red score down her muzzle where Nailbiter had delicately nicked her.

The stallion and other mare caught the scent of blood, and Sam saw their eyes flashing. They were breathing more heavily now, and their wings were in an aggressive, half-out-and-up position, making the beasts look bigger than they already were.

That's when Sam realized her battle senses weren't complete. When she'd fought with Leeta, she'd always *felt* where each of her enemies were, as if she and her shieldmate were able to somehow share their senses with each other. She knew it wasn't anything so mystical, but rather than complete trust they had in each other, and the 'marks and 'marks of practice and experience they'd shared. But here in the village green, *it was missing.* As the pegasi separated, Sam was forced to swivel her head back and forth in an attempt to keep track of them all.

Her left foot slid out from under her as she stepped in some uncollected pegasus excrement, and she cursed softly as she scrambled to recover. The stallion had taken a quick step forward, but it slowly moved back as Sam waved Nailbiter in front of it. As she scanned for the mare on her right, she saw the half-elf Alred step out of the dry good shop with a heavy bow in one hand. "Alred, don't," she warned. "It'll just make them angrier." Then she saw Dardrad hurry to the edge of the walkway carrying a heavy battle axe. "Yeah," she said more softly to herself, "that'll be useful, if it comes to it."

A pounding that she felt as much as heard announced Warren's arrival, and when the three pegasi looked up and took another step backwards, she risked a quick turn of her head to see what he'd brought. Her eyes widened as she realized that his giant crossbow was in fact a wagon-mounted ballista that he was simply carrying in one hand. "Hold, Warren," she cautioned. "Unless you hit one straight in the chest, it'll go through and hit someone behind."

"It's just in case," the ogre assured her.

"Sam," a gravelly voice said as a lighter person ran up behind her. Jen.

Suddenly, the village green—the *battlefield*, in Sam's mind—snapped into place. The stallion in *front*, and Sam continued to make small adjustments to her stance to keep him centered before her. One mare three paces *left*, the other four paces *right*, directly in front of the concerned-looked dwarf. Warren behind and slightly to her left, Jen now stepping up to her right. A rush of cold air announced the appearance of her arm-armor, and a *hiss* of air told Sam that Jen had summoned Hellsting.

Sam's mouth twitched into a bit of a grin at the name.

Arrayed around the walkway were—Dexter, she realized with some surprise, and a quick glance to her left showed he'd brought a medic's bag and was slowly making his way around to Prudence. Galhani was in front of the tea shop, walking to offer support to Leota, who'd risen and was holding the back of the chair Sam had been using. The dryads were just now stepping out of their shop. Rhys', the potter's husband, was telling his wife—who'd wisely remained indoors—what was happening, and helping Cole with Prudence and Bryant. Makota was standing in the doorway to her bakery, eyes wide.

Sam's battle-calm settled over her. Everything felt sharp and new, and the world seemed to slow, giving her more time to consider her options and take action. "Still against violence, I assume?" Sam joked to Jen.

She snorted. "Nominally, yes, but if they can't stay in peace. . ."

"Think we could take them?"

Jen considered, even as the mare in front of her lunged again, screaming a challenge. Jen took a step forward, whirling her weapon in a complicated dance before her. The mare pulled up, rearing slightly and yanking her head out of the way. At that exact moment, the stallion snapped his wings shut, and Sam turned to her right to meet the second mare, already charging with her head down. *If I don't stop her, she'll plow into Jen,* Sam thought cooly. Instead of diving to one side and striking the pegasus' left flank, she managed a standing jump, coming down just as the beast's head arrived. She used her momentum to smash her sword's pommel into the mare's skull, leaving a bloody gash and sending the horse stumbling back, shaking its head and spreading its wings further in confusion. *I am going to pay for that,* Sam thought ruefully as her back complained about the unaccustomed effort.

The stallion neighed twice.

The mares turned to look at him, and then—seemingly with some reluctance—lowered their wings back to their flanks.

"That's it," Sam said heavily. "They're giving up. For now." Nailbiter vanished with a *thwick,* and another rush of cool air told her that Jen's weapon was gone as well. "Warren, take that thing back to your smithy, and I'm going to want the tale of why you have it later," Sam called. "Everyone else, back inside. Show them we're leaving them alone."

"For now," Jen muttered.

The stallion pointedly began grazing again, and after a moment the mares wandered out of their fighting position and joined him.

"Cole," Jen called as the grocer began making his way back to his shop, "did you get what you need for our little idea?"

"I did," he called back. "Galhani helped me figure out how to spray it."

Jen clapped Sam on the back. "Let's go see if Vamir has a book on the subject."

fifteen

. . .

"I'VE BEEN LOOKING," Vamir sighed, staring down one long row of packed shelves. "But you know the trick of this place, Jen."

"I thought it always had the book you needed?" Sam asked.

"Well, as far as we know, it does," Vamir said. "Although I've never used it for things *we* need, just for travelers. But the *trick* of it is actually *finding* the book. I know it's in here. I can sense it." He shrugged. "It's a little mischievous. Poly!"

Sam raised an eyebrow as some sort of scuffle started in the back of the shop. The noise seemed to rush toward where they were standing in the front, and she took a step backwards as. . . *something* burst into the clear space in front of the shelves. It leapt to Vamir's shoulder.

As it settled, Sam realized it was some kind of. . . bird? It seemed feathery, although now that it was starting to preen itself, that mass of white feathers—fur?—were laying down a bit, making it seem less like a ball of puff and more like a. . . *children's toy?* "Um," she said.

Vamir laughed, the hearty, sunlight-on-water laugh that only forest elves could manage. It seemed to brighten the room. "This is Polyocular. Poly, for short. Poly, say hello to Sam."

The creature's entire body seemed to swivel toward Sam as it cracked its stubby beak and squawked, "Dah-ay-loh oo-tye!" It slowly blinked its huge blue eyes and then opened what Sam realized was a third eye, set up and between the first two.

"Um," Sam repeated. "Is it a bird?"

"No?" Vamir chuckled. "Sort of? She can't fly, although she does have these stubby little wing-arms." Poly flapped these now as if to demonstrate. "And her feet are certainly birdlike, although they're. . . fuzzy." Poly tilted her body to one side so that she could extend what was indeed a white-fuzzed foot that mimicked the shape of a large bird's claw.

"She's intelligent," Sam noted.

"Very. And she's usually a tremendous help in finding the book I'm searching for. But we've struggled, this time. I don't think she has a concept for what a pegasus is, and she refuses to leave the shop so I can show her."

"Where did you find her?"

"Oh, she came with the shop, when I arrived," the elf said easily. "Poly." The creature turned to focus on him, its third eye closing and the other two blinking slowly. "Dah moh-moh doo-ay-loo-lah?"

Poly blinked again a few times, and then leapt from Vamir's shoulder. Its fur—features?—puffed out, doubling its apparent size, and seemed to help it float quickly to the floor. It scurried off—faster than Sam would have thought possible, given its stubby legs—and vanished into the shelves. "Doesn't stop us looking ourselves, but she seems to have a knack for it, usually. Take a shelf."

Vamir, Sam, and Jen each spread out. Sam began running her finger over book spines, methodically looking for anything that seemed related to pegasi.

After a candlemark—with Sam's back complaining bitterly about not having a lie-down after all its exertion—Galhani eased into the shop, carrying a tray set with tea service. "Thought you could all benefit from this. I call it 'Puruwhero.' Should help perk you up a bit and keep you alert."

"How'd you know we were in here?" Sam asked.

Galhani smiled. "The shops all talk, dear."

At exactly that moment, Sam felt an irresistible urge to be in the pub. "Duty calls," she groaned.

"Go, go," Galhani said. "I'll help with the lower shelves for a bit."

Sam left, casting a longing look at the sharp-smelling pot of tea, and set off toward the main gate. She paused when she saw Cole and his eldest, Senan, standing just off the walkway in front of the grocery. They were frowning, and were each carrying what looked like oversized watering cans. Their glares seemed directed at the pegasi, who were munching grass with unusual energy. "Cole," she called. "What's up?"

"An idea Jen had," Cole called back. He and his son stepped back onto the walkway, which the pegasi had seemed to acknowledge as human territory. "She thought if we could make an infusion of the hottest peppers we could find, and then sprinkle it on the grass, that the pegasi wouldn't like it."

Sam cocked an eyebrow. "They seem to have a taste for strong flavors."

"Sam, that stuff all but burned a hole through my regular watering can!" Cole complained. "Galhani helped us come up with a coating that resists it for a while. But they love it!"

"I guess we'll try something else," Sam said, shaking her head and breaking into a jog as the pub's summons prodded her again.

It was already late in the afternoon, but it seemed as if every traveler on the road had made an extra effort to get to North Pointe Common Towne before evening. Sam hadn't initially expected any travelers at all today, but more than a dozen sets began arriving just minutes after she threw open the pub's doors.

Treasure seekers. "Don't know that I've heard that particular legend, but that's goblin territory. Going to want to make sure you have good, light armor, trust me. Stop by Mistral Adventures, just down the road, and Tyran will get you equipped."

Knows where they're going, hint of personal. "So sorry to hear about your brother. Did he have kids? Oh, that's a shame. Tell you what, since you're spending the night, stop at the herbalist's shop. She'll give you something to help you sleep, so you can get an early start."

Personal, tastes like revenge. "Well, just don't do anything you'll regret later. Is that. . . er, the sword you're planning to use? I mean, yeah, if you're interested, the smithy is just across the road. I'm sure Warren would be happy to see what he has available. He's an ogre, mind you, but he's as friendly as anyone here."

Personal, feels. . . really weird. "To where? For. . . why?" *Oh, gods above.* "Well, I thank you kindly for the compliment, but that's just not my speed, and I'm very comfortable here, thanks. You know, you might want to stop at the chirgeon's, I'm sure he can offer you something in the way of. . . you know. *Protection.* Before you get there. But. . . definitely enjoy yourselves." *I had no idea river elves were so. . . frisky.*

When the pub had called so urgently, Sam had half-hoped that today would be the day she'd find a new villager. Maybe another grizzled old campaigner who could teach fighting classes. Maybe a legendary horse-trainer who could get the stupid pegasi to leave. Anything. But the ball in the pub's device never even hesitated as each group stepped in, flying immediately into one of the colored areas. Nothing at all to suggest any of these people should be urged to spend a night at Minnie's. Not that she'd have room—she'd already rushed over to inform Sam that she had just the one tiny room left, good for two if they were *very* comfortable with each other, anyone else was going to need to bed down in their own wagons or camp outside the gates.

The ball stayed roughly centered as the next traveler stepped in, and Sam's eyes lowered as her heart pounded a bit faster in anticipation. Then her shoulders slumped as she realized the man was dressed as a minstrel. *Still, first we've had since I got here.*

"Any chance," he began with a friendly smile.

"Free board for up to—" she paused, listening for the pub. *A sennight,* it responded. "—a sennight. I can't offer you a better room than one of these benches for the night, but if something frees up at the inn, it's yours. There's actually a small room empty, so if nobody takes it by sundown, you're in. Music from noon to four 'marks past, quarter-mark breaks every 'mark. Then we'll feed you, and music with breaks for another four 'marks after."

The man blinked a few times. "You've done this before."

Sam shrugged. "Standard terms." Indeed, Nate had drilled them into her during the first sennight. "And honestly, you won't find a safer or friendlier town around the Mistrals. And if you care to play later, you'll get a decent custom from the locals. Haven't had one of you through yet this season. Oh, and any tips are yours to keep. Happy to supply you with small beer during the day, ale in the evenings, so long as you can pace yourself."

"I don't enjoy ale, actually," he said, smiling politely, "but if you've a nontoxic red wine of some kind, a glass will usually see me through the evening."

"We actually have some excellent stuff," Sam said brightly. "That I never get an excuse to open, which is a shame because I'm partial to it myself. Done."

"Done and done," the man grinned. "I'll just get set up, then."

It wasn't long before a gentle, pleasant strumming filled the pub, spilling outside and inviting people in.

"We found it," Jen said, striding into the pub and slapping a thin volume onto the bar. "Oh, you got a musicker. Excellent." She listened for a moment and then nodded. "He's not bad."

Orcs: Lore, Myth, and Truth, the hand-lettered cover said. *From the Mistrals to the Mountedives.* "Anything useful?" Sam asked.

Jen frowned. "Just this." She flipped the book open and thumped a particular passage. Sam quickly scanned it. "Orcs?" she said with disgust. "That's the only thing they're afraid of? Orcs?"

"Terrified, apparently," Jen said drily.

"So we just need to go get a pet orc."

"That's it."

"That's not helpful."

"Not particularly, no."

Orcs were huge, powerful creatures—bigger than orges, and absolutely insular. They hated *all* other sentient species. They barely tolerated each other. Left to themselves, they'd happily occupy freezing mountain reaches that no other species could inhabit. Until, that is, something came over them. Nobody had ever figured out exactly what it took—lack of forage, existential anger, position of the stars—but they'd occasionally take it into their heads to march down whatever mountain they'd claimed and lay waste to the first settlement they came across. They'd eat everything that couldn't get away, set fire to the remains, and march back up their mountain.

It was the main reason orc-hunting quests were encouraged. They were seen as a kind of preventative measure, if not preemptory strikes.

"So what now?" Sam asked.

"I don't know, I—" Jen stopped and turned as a pair of young men stepped in.

"Greetings-travelers-welcome-to-the-Broken-Claw-how-may-I-serve," Sam said automatically. Her eyes flicked up and widened as the ball shot into Heroic Quest and stayed there, vibrating slightly as if in emphasis.

"A meal would be grand," the one man—tall, slender, white hair, narrow blue eyes, perfect skin, *He'd make an elf blush with jealousy,* Sam thought—said. "And a room, if one exists, although we'd honestly be happy with anything inside walls for a night."

"We'll be off at first light," the second—a fraction shorter, far more heavily built, brown hair, green eyes—added. "We're planning to head up into the Mistrals in the morning."

"And if you have an outfitter by any stroke of luck," White Hair said, "we've a few items we've been unable to acquire elsewhere."

"What," Jen said carefully, "are you planning to do in the Mistrals?" There weren't many options, Sam knew, and she held her breath for the answer.

"Hunt orcs," Brown Hair said bluntly.

"We need to chat," Sam blurted out.

———

"Shame there's not a bounty on pegasi," D'norle—formerly known as White Hair—mused. "But half the kingdoms think they're mythical and the other half think they're endangered. I didn't know about the orc thing, though."

Sam, Jen, and the two travelers had taken a table near the bar. Sam kept an eye on the door, but the evening traffic seemed to have petered out. Most of the travelers in the pub were enjoying a bowl of Minnie's stew, although she kept scanning the tables to see if anyone needed more ale.

"We passed a farm out east that had been overrun by them," N'rogara—Brown Hair—said. "Like, literally overrun. What they didn't eat, they trampled. Folks there had given up and moved on, and woe betide if you so much as stepped off the main road into the fields. There must have been two dozen of them, and they'd come running at you, heads down and mouths open. Filthy beasts. Although it's not like you can just lure an orc down here."

The two men had introduced themselves as Rohanian Wayfarers. Sam had heard of them, but never met one and didn't know much about them. "We're basically like Elysian Rangers," D'norle said with a wide grin, "but without the religious fervor or central management. We just kind of wander where we want to, looking for quests that will help people."

"By killing orcs?" Jen asked wryly.

He shrugged. "A dead orc is an orc that won't come tromping out of the mountains to burn your village and eat your neighbors."

"Plus, several of the little kingdoms to the east and west offer substantial bounties," N'rogara added.

"They should worry about orcs becoming extinct, not pegasi," Sam muttered.

"Never happen," N'rogara said, shaking his head. "Do you know how those things reproduce?"

"I. . ." Sam ventured, and then realized she might not want to know.

"After they've had a big meal—think an entire village or so—they go back and *lay eggs*. No actual mating, since they can barely stand to be within a league of one another. But they can lay *dozens*. None of which will hatch until mommy/daddy has been gone for a good long while. And the eggs keep for *decades*. The Mistrals alone probably have hundreds of unborn orcs just waiting for enough alone time to hatch."

"That's disgusting," Jen frowned.

"That's terrifying," Sam added.

"That's why we're heading up tomorrow. You can get a bounty for the eggs too, although there's a certain amount of danger. You get about a sennight to show your proof and then burn it before it hatches."

"Four hells," Jen muttered.

"I wonder," Sam mused, "if an egg would do it? Like, if that'd be enough smell, or whatever, to drive the pegasi off?"

Jen's frown deepened. "Dangerous, though. If the thing hatches. . . orcs aren't easy to take down."

"Yeah, I'm not sure I'd recommend that approach," D'norle said, thinking it through. "Even assuming we could get it down in two days, that'd only leave you five at the outside, four to be safe, and your book doesn't mention how long it actually takes."

"What about a skin?" N'rogara suggested.

"You mean. . . kill one, and take its skin?" Sam asked.

"No," D'norle said. "They have to age for *moons* before you can get the skin off. But you could grab one they've shed."

"Shed." Jen blinked a few times in confusion.

"Sure," N'rogara said. "They're constantly growing. That's why the older ones are so much more dangerous. They can get to twice a man's height, and weigh two, even three hundred stone. Just monstrous. But their skin doesn't grow with them. They outgrow their skin about every five years or so, and they just shed the old one."

"Best time to get one, actually," D'norle put in. "Just after they've shed. The new skin is pretty soft and vulnerable for about a sennight, and then it toughens up."

"Orc skin," Sam said, having trouble processing the concept.

"Absolutely," D'norle said confidently. "They smell *just* like a live orc. Really hold the smell, actually," he added, wrinkling his nose. "But the good news is they tend to leave them in piles near their cave entrances. Wonderful way to make sure everything in the vicinity knows to stay away. But it makes them relatively easy to take, if that's what you're after."

"You know," N'rogara said thoughtfully, "we're planning to spend a few sennights up in the Mistrals. But if you have someone willing to go with us, we could help them secure a skin, and then they could head straight back down to help deal with your pegasus problem."

Go, the pub whispered to Sam.

"I think," she said slowly, her eyes meeting Jen's across the table, "I volunteer."

sixteen

. . .

THE WIND *sure blows cold up here,* Sam thought grimly as she stepped over a chunk of ice-covered rock.

"It's always this cold up here," D'norle called back softly, as if reading her mind. "Doesn't matter the season, somehow."

They'd set out at first light, not even bothering to travel further down the trade road. They'd simply walked through the village's road gates, past the wooden stockade of the small farm, and up into the foothills of the Mistrals.

The first five or six candlemarks had been not only unremarkable, they'd been *dull.* As the sun had poked its head over the western horizon, the Mistrals had revealed themselves to be craggy, inhospitable, and even inimical. N'rogara was apparently the most experienced with this environment, because he was the one who'd pointed out the many dangers to avoid as they climbed.

"Thrushthorn," he'd point out not long after they'd begun hiking upward. It was an innocent-looking brush with brown leaves and deep red berries. "Keep at least an arm's length from it," he'd advised, "because it'll lash out and entangle your feet faster than you can blink."

"You're kidding," Sam had said in disbelief.

By way of answer, he'd simply picked up a rock and tossed it next to the bush. Instantly, a dozen or more brown branches had thrust out, berries shaking violently. They'd wrapped themselves around the rock and yanked it into the center of the bush. It had all, as promised, taken just an eyeblink. "They're carnivorous," he'd said with a shrug. "The smell of the berries is attractive to a lot of smaller animals, and then it just drags them in."

"Gods."

"Hear that chirping?" he'd said a half 'mark or so later.

"Birds?" Sam guessed.

"No, but you're meant to think so. It's actually a tree. We're still low enough down that some of the animals from below will venture up here. That tree attracts smaller predators."

"And then sucks them in and eats them?"

"Exactly. They'll make a play at humans if you get too close, but they're not strong enough to actually pull one of us up. A small child, maybe."

"Good reason not to let small children play in the Mistrals," Sam quipped.

D'norle snorted.

Not long after, something white and furry had bounded across the rough path they'd been following.

"Didn't expect rabbits up here," Sam said, panting a bit with effort by then.

"That," N'rogara said with humor, "was not a rabbit."

"Was it a carnivorous bunny that eats humans in their sleep?" Sam asked.

He chuckled. "No, they're actually vegetarian and quite intelligent. They're called tchoup-tchoups. They actually *do* look a lot like rabbits, at first glance," he admitted, "but they're incredibly mischievous. That one will probably follow us for a while to see if it can play some kind of prank on us."

"A prank."

He nodded. "Lure us off the path, usually by making attractive sounds. They're excellent mimics. We'll have to watch this trail, too, they've been known to create new ones that lead nowhere and then block the main trail."

"You're joking."

"'Fraid not. But, sometimes they'll take a liking to someone. They make great companions, once you get to know one."

They'd clumped along in relative silence for another half 'mark or so before Sam asked, "So where exactly did this trail come from? Doesn't seem like a lot of people go hiking up here for pleasure."

"Oh, definitely not. It's mainly from larger animals. There's a species of ruminant up here, really similar to highelk, called lopers. Incredibly fast and agile when they need to be, but for the most part they just wander around browsing for food. They can eat almost any of the vegetation up here, even thrushthorn. But if you look, these paths are also where a lot of the snowmelt runs. This scrubby grassy stuff grows really quickly when the ground is wet, and they're aggressive about letting other plants take root. So the path stays relatively easy."

"I'm surprised anything melts up here," Sam said, pulling her heavy coat tighter around her. Tyran had been generous in equipping them for the trek, and his shop had turned up—as advertised—exactly what they'd needed.

"Mostly in summer, maybe a moon or two from now," D'norle put in. "It's actually more dangerous then than at any time. Some of these paths get flooded pretty quickly, and then you're forced to move up to the ridges." He gestured to one side, and Sam realized that the narrow path they'd been following was actually at the center of a ravine as wide as a house.

"Wait, this whole *thing* floods?"

"Oh, definitely. Probably a handful of times every year. Snow melts lower down, creates a flood of water. That lets the higher snow pack slide down a bit, where it melts, and so on. The only reason your village doesn't flood out every year is that these ravines all join up lower down. That little river that runs to the west of your gate is all fed by this."

"Amazing."

"From here," N'rogara cautioned, "we should probably speak more softly. Orcs don't have great ears, but voices carry in weird ways up here, with the wind and the rock."

Sam had nodded acknowledgement, and they'd continued climbing. Now, a handful of candlemarks later, the terrain had grown rougher and rockier. They navigated through narrow crevasses, and came across more than a few large-mouthed caves. These, the Wayfarers inspected closely and carefully, with Sam standing a good ways back. All had proven to be empty. "We're still low down," N'rogara said with a shrug. "Didn't expect these to be occupied, but it's worth checking."

"The worst thing you can do is continue on and leave a live orc behind you," D'norle agreed.

The sun was cresting past noon when N'rogara, in the front of their small group, suddenly stopped and crouched low. He made some quick hand signs to D'norle, who turned and signaled Sam to back up. She did so slowly, and as quietly as she could manage, her boots rustling softly in the omnipresent tan scrub.

The two men huddled around her. "Likely cave ahead," N'rogara whispered.

"You can see it?" Sam whispered back.

He shook his head. "No, but there are some moderately fresh corpses here. Orc-sign. Nothing else is trying to pick at them, and the orc will save it until it's ripe enough to stop smelling. They like their food aged, and everything else around here knows better than to try and help themselves."

"That means we'll be within a few hundred feet of its cave," D'norle said. "They don't store food inside, but they don't stack it up too far, either."

"We'll move forward slowly," N'rogara instructed. "Stay about ten paces behind us, but don't lose sight of D'norle's back. *Don't* touch the corpses. Don't even brush them as you pass. If we find the orc, you'll know—they're not subtle beasts."

"Can we just grab the skin and run?" Sam asked.

N'rogara shook his head. "No, for two reasons. One, it'll smell us and come out to fight whether we want it to or not. Two," he added with a grin, "there's a hefty bounty on these things."

"Ever seen an orc? Or even a sketch of one?" D'norle asked. Sam shook her head. "They're terrifying. In fact, there's a legend that says they were created by magic, ages and ages ago, and that they were *designed* to be terrifying. Don't let it get to you."

"Okay," Sam said. She'd never been afraid to be afraid, and she was definitely feeling nervous right now. She ran a thumb across Nailbiter's hilt.

N'rogara noticed and nodded approvingly. "Use your weapon, if you can. Just know that their skin—unless it's just shed recently—is like leather over rock. The softest spots, and only relatively speaking, are their throats and under their arms. If you think you can get an eye, drive deep—they've a bone plate behind their eye sockets that protects their brains. If you don't go all the way through, you'll just make it madder. Don't bother hacking at its limbs, it won't even notice."

"My sword is pretty. . . sharp," Sam said.

He raised an eyebrow. "Well, feel free to try. But the more you can aim for a soft spot, the faster it'll be over. Hang back as much as you can and watch us—we've done this more than a few times."

"Okay."

"Quiet from here," he instructed.

Sam nodded, and the two men turned and began creeping forward.

The wind was blowing in their faces, rushing down the mountain like an invisible avalanche, and Sam hoped that meant they'd have an advantage in terms of an orc picking up their scent. Cold as she was, Sam was pretty sure she couldn't possibly emit any scent to begin with, but N'rogara had assured her that orcs had incredibly keen senses of smell.

As they edged around a clump of bushes—Sam quickly checked to make sure they didn't look like any of the attacking varieties the men had pointed out on the climb—her nose wrinkled a moment before her eyes spotted the rotting, half-eaten body. It was some kind of four-legged wild animal—akin to one of the large plains cats, she thought, or maybe one of the hill country coyotes. The smell was relatively mild, meaning it had been killed a sennight or more ago. In air this frigid, it'd certainly keep a while, and with winds this strong, not even flies buzzed around.

She gave the thing as wide a berth as she could, mindful of N'rogara's warning.

Ahead of her, the two men stopped behind a large boulder. D'norle turned and waved her forward. She scuttled to them, hunching low. D'norle pointed two fingers to his eyes, and then pointed the same fingers around the boulder. Sam eased sideways a bit and spotted it: a low, wide-mouthed opening in the rock. Heaped just inside it was a pile of. . . *leather?* She turned back to D'norle, who smiled and pinched the skin of his arm. *Gross,* Sam thought, taking one last look at the pile of shed skins before easing herself fully behind the boulder.

N'rogara leaned close, placing his lips directly against her ear to whisper, "It's dangerous to go in, so we have to lure it out."

Sam nodded enthusiastically. Going in sounded like a terrible idea. She gave an exaggerated shrug: *How?*

"Remember I told you not to touch the corpse?"

Again, Sam nodded, then her eyes grew wide. N'rogara pulled away and met her stare with a grin that reminded her of Nate's: lopsided and casual. It seemed wholly inappropriate for the current scenario.

The two men stepped slowly around the boulder, gradually easing out of their crouch until they were standing upright. N'rogara gently eased a massive broadsword out of the sheath on his back, while D'norle produced a small but powerful-looking crossbow from under his cloak. He fitted it with what looked like a steel bolt, tensioned the string, and then nodded to his companion.

N'rogara looked back at Sam, who was peeking over the boulder, and nodded to her. Then he nodded to the corpse, before looking back to her.

Oh, me, she thought, nodding once. She waited until his attention returned to the cave entrance, and then cast about for a rock. She found a fist-sized one at the base of her boulder, picked it up, and lobbed it at the corpse.

It landed with a *thunk.*

Huh, she thought after a moment's silence. *Guess I'll need to find—*

Her thought was interrupted by the most profoundly terrible howl she'd ever experienced. Sam had *seen* orcs before, often at a safe distance while someone else tried to take them down, but she'd never heard one roar like that. The sound rattled her organs, and she found herself pushing more firmly into the boulder in some purely instinctual effort to hide. Part of her brain clamored for her to *get away!* while another urged her to try and dig a hole of some kind that she could crawl into. She clenched her jaw against both instincts and reached for Nail-biter's hilt.

The roar cut off, and was followed by a deep, powerful, rhythmic vibration. *It's running,* she realized. *Galloping toward us.*

The pounding lasted for all of four heartbeats before the orc burst from the mouth of its cave, roaring in fury.

Still peeking over the top of the bolder, Sam forced herself to remain still, because her brain's two voices had finally agreed that *run the four hells away* was the right message, and she was getting it loud and clear.

This orc was *massive.*

Like all of its kind, it ran on four legs, like some kind of supersized bear. Its gray skin was mottled, gnarled, and clearly not at all soft and new. Enormous yellowed tusks protruded upwards from is lower jaw, and thick, viscous spittle flew and dripped as it screamed its rage. Its black, beady eyes, set deeply beneath a horny ridge, locked onto the two Wayfarers at once.

Roaring again, it rose to its rear legs.

Sam's jaw clamped even harder as she forced herself to remain still. Orcs were motion-centric, and to move now would be to attract its attention from the two men, who'd spaced themselves out so that the orc couldn't attack them both at once. But this is where orcs became their most terrifying.

The thing's forelegs cracked and popped as they extended, its thick, clawed fingers lengthening into true fingers. Its skin stretched, becoming more taut across its enormous, deeply muscled frame. Its rear legs extended as well, although not as far, and its knee and hip joints made sickening, sinewy noises as they shifted to accommodate the beast's immense weight.

With a *thwack*, D'norle loosed a bolt toward the thing's eye. But a last minute twitch of its thick neck muscles sent the bolt careening off the horny eye ridge. The force was enough to rock the orc's head back slightly, and it howled even louder as it fixed on the taller of its opponents.

Then it charged.

N'rogara dove right, swinging his massive sword in a circle to build momentum. D'norle dove left, and the orc followed. N'rogara brought his sword down hard on the back of the creature's left knee, obviously trying to find a weaker spot amongst all the wrist-thick tendons that bunched there. It wasn't enough to cut the thing, but the force was enough to throw it off its stride, and it went down to one knee, its outstretched right hand passing within a hair's breadth of D'norle's head.

The taller man had somehow managed to reload his crossbow, and another bolt flew, again missing the orc's eye but this time managing to pierce the thick hide of its cheek. N'rogara had pulled his sword back and, now gripping it in two hands, whirled it around, leapt into the air, and brought the blade down on the back of the orc's neck.

The monster bellowed again, spittle flying over the boulder

and streaking wet and hot across Sam's cheek. "Ugh!" she said without thinking.

The orc's tiny eyes snapped to her.

"Uh, oh."

It lunged forward, ignoring the two armed men to its sides, and reached over the boulder to grab her.

Sam twisted quickly, rising to her right from her crouch. As the orc's arms reached for her, Nailbiter's blade appeared with a *schnick* and, quick as thought, Sam sliced at the orc's left arm. She caught it mid-forearm, and her arms shuddered as Nailbiter bit a half-thumblength into the boulder. The orc's hand and wrist dropped to the ground, green blood spurting and steaming in the cold air.

The creature pulled back, grabbed its arm with its remaining hand, reared its head back, and let out a. . . there was no word for it. It was a *sound*, certainly, but it pierced more than just the ears. Sam fell backwards as the physical *force* of the thing's outburst struck her in the chest. Her ears shut down in self-defense, filling her mind with a sharp ringing noise.

D'norle dropped his crossbow, crouched, laced his fingers together, and held them at knee height. N'rogara was already in motion, leaping to place one booted foot in his companion's hands. D'norle stood, flinging his arms upward to boost N'rogara's leap. It sent the shorter man more than his own height into the air, his sword held straight up—

—where it plunged into the orc's neck, directly behind its chin at the base of its jaw.

The sword *thunked* to a halt, unable to pierce through the top of the creature's heavy skull, but it didn't need to. N'rogara released his sword hilt and scrambled backwards as the orc began to topple. D'norle rolled to one side, ignoring his crossbow in an effort to get out of the way as quickly as possible.

The orc fell backwards, pushed just over the tipping point by the force of N'rogara's killing blow. It crashed hard enough to bounce Sam off the ground.

Everyone lay still on the ground for several moments, staring at the monstrous killing machine with a sword still protruding from its neck. Slowly, Sam's ears stopped ringing, and the quiet rush of wind came back to her.

"Wow," D'norle said, finally recovering enough to stand. "Your sword *is* sharp."

"Changeling weapon?" N'rogara asked, standing and brushing himself off. He eyed his sword and sighed. "I'm going to need some help with that. I felt like the tip might have lodged in its skull."

"Yeah," Sam said, dismissing the blade with a *thwick* and hanging the hilt at her belt. "Let's give it a pull."

They stood atop the orc, bracing themselves against its head and chest, and eventually managed to tug the sword free. N'rogara immediately started cleaning it, using a cloth he produced from a pocket, a bit of water from his canteen, and a good deal of dirt scraped up from the ground. "Their blood is mildly acidic, and the dirt helps neutralize it," he explained. "Do you need to. . .?"

Sam shook her head. "No, she cleans herself when the blade vanishes."

"Convenient."

"Very. So I take it these are the skins?" she said, nodding to the cave mouth.

N'rogara looked at the pile of not-leather. "Yeah. I'd thought to maybe give you one and stick with you about halfway down, but there's no way. We're going to have to cut one up between us to get it down."

D'norle stepped into the cave and emerged a few moments later. "There's a pile of eggs," he said happily. "Wasn't the king of Kithwellen willing to take the husks instead of the whole things?"

"Yeah, if we can crack them open," N'rogara said, sheathing his sword. "Sam, if you don't mind helping, actually, that sword of yours. . ."

"Consider it done," Sam said. "I'm assuming you two are still good giving me the skin for free, and you keep all the bounties?"

"Oh, indeed," D'norle confirmed with a grin.

Sam smiled tiredly as she unhooked Nailbiter's hilt. "Show me where to slice."

———

The sun was a down a candle mark by the time they trudged back into town. They'd taken empty nets up with them—Tyran's shop had more or less insisted on it—and filled them with orc-egg husks and pieces of the creature's skin.

"You know," Sam remarked as Warren rushed out to help them unload their burdens, "even down here it the warmth, it doesn't smell of anything to me."

"Me either," Warren said, lifting a heavy piece of hide and sniffing it. "And I've got a better sense of smell than humans."

"Hopefully the pegasi will find it especially revolting," Sam said, staring doubtfully at the pile of thick, wrinkled skin.

"We had an idea when you were gone," a female voice said. Sam turned to see Prudence, her withering frown now focused on the admittedly gross-looking orc skin. "But I think I'd better work out here," she said. "Instead of trying to carry it back to my shop."

"You can use the smithy," Warren said. "I've got the frame ready."

"Frame?" Sam asked.

Prudence looked up, met Sam's eyes, and her frown vanished. In fact. . . Sam thought she might actually be attempting a *smile*. "Like I told you," the seamstress said, "we had an idea."

seventeen

. . .

"PRUDENCE," Sam said quietly, stepping into the smithy, "can I have a quick word?"

Everyone had helped haul the heavy orc skin into the smithy, and followed Prudence's instructions for spreading it out on one of Warren's broad work tables. She'd *tskd* a few times at the way the largely intact skin had been cut up, but D'norle and N'rogara had simply shrugged, excused themselves, and headed to the Weary Head for the evening. They'd already told Sam they planned to head back into the Mistrals the next day to continue hunting for orcs, and after a fairly protracted attempt to convince her to join them, they'd finally given up and decided to have some stew and call it a night.

"What is it?" the seamstress snapped, turning to Sam with her hands on her hips.

"First of all," Sam said, forcing her tone to remain gentle, "how's Bryant?"

Prudence's iron-hard expression relaxed a bit. "He's okay. He's fine, actually. I. . . thank you." Her shoulders slumped a bit as she relaxed even further. "Really, thank you. You had no reason. . . I mean, you don't owe me—"

"We take care of each other," Sam said. "Serve all, right? That includes us." Prudence nodded slowly. "Prudence, have I done anything. . . to upset you? To offend? If so, I'd very much like to know, so that I can—"

"No," Prudence said with an explosive breath, shaking her head. "No, it's me." She raised her eyes to the stone roof for a moment, gathering herself before she once again met Sam's eyes. "It's me. I can tell. . . look, you're obviously perfect for each other. And for this place. Where I come from. . . it's just considered. . . and you know, it shouldn't matter, they're the ones—"

"Slow down, slow down," Sam said, her brown wrinkling in concern as the younger woman began speaking faster. "I don't even know what you're talking about. Who's a perfect fit?"

Prudence fell silent, her eyes widening. "Oh," she said after a moment. "I thought. . . well, it's not my place. I mean. . ." she sighed again. "You don't know much about me, do you?"

"Honestly, everyone's been very protective of your privacy," Sam said. "I know next to nothing."

Prudence nodded very slowly, and then leaned back against the work table. "Well, you should. I come from a place pretty far away from here. Have you ever heard of Holderdown?"

Sam's eyes widened. "Yes, but. . . wow, that *is* far away." Then she frowned a bit. "Aren't they. . . fairly conservative, out there?"

Prudence snorted and rolled her eyes. "'Fairly' is the understatement of the century, but yes." Then her eyes grew distant. "I married young. Normal age, for our people, but young everywhere else, I realized. His name was Aleks. We. . . he truly did love me. Our marriage was arranged by our parents—it's all negotiation for money and influence, back home, but we truly did love one another. Byrant was born in love," she said more softly, a gentle smile settling onto her lips. But it faded quickly. "He was killed," she said simply, wrapping her arms around herself. "It was in a bandit raid."

"I'm sorry."

"Thank you. I still miss him, you know. And Bryant will

never even know him." She fell silent for a long moment, and Sam stood still until she was ready to continue. "Unmarried women aren't a. . . *thing,* where I come from. And so my parents immediately started negotiations."

Sam felt her ire rise. "You're joking."

Prudence shook her head. "I am not. They'd decided on a man four times my age—an *old* man, Sam. I would have been his *fifth* wife. Bryant and I would have had shelter, would have been fed, but I'd have been little more than an unpaid servant. 'Slave' is a filthy word, even where I come from, but. . . it wouldn't have been inaccurate."

"Gods," Sam whispered.

Prudence gave her a wan smile. "So I ran."

"With. . . four hells, woman, with a *baby?*"

"I wasn't. . . as well-informed, back then. This was a couple of years ago, obviously. I've. . . I'd like to think I've grown a little. But yes. With a baby, whatever I could carry on my own back, and the sturdiest boots I could make fit."

"And you came here."

"Not at first. The villages to the south. . . there just wasn't a place for me. Most were generous, they'd feed us and let us sleep for a couple of nights. Help get me better equipped. But you know how it is along the lake. You have to pull your own weight. Without a husband. . ."

Sam nodded. She'd seen it all too often when a husband was killed, or even injured to the point where he couldn't work. "That happened to a woman in my village, when I was young," she said quietly. "I was. . . gods, maybe sixteen. I'd already been learning to fight, but that's when I decided I wouldn't stay. I wouldn't be. . . *subject* to that. I needed to make my own way. Merc companies, they don't care what kind of equipment you're packing. Women get an even field. Although babies. . ."

"Not an option," Prudence grinned. The expression didn't last. "But I'd already had Bryant," she shrugged. "And without a trade, without a way to make money. . ."

"Yeah."

"But eventually I came here. It was the usual thing at first—everyone took pity on us. We—"

"I'm sure it wasn't pity," Sam said quickly.

"I'm not ashamed of being pitied," Prudence said firmly. "Bryant and I have lived on charity for much of his life, and I'm not ashamed. I'm committed to paying it back to others, whenever I can. Being able to help other people who can't help themselves, for the moment. . . back home, they tell us that's the gods' way." She snorted softly. "They don't practice it, but *I* can."

"I imagine," Sam said slowly, "you were a good fit here."

"I was," Prudence said with a hard smile. "They'd had a tailor, in the past, and I fit right in. More work than you'd think, especially since I'm good with leather work. Better than I was when I came, in fact. That's. . . I think it's a gift of my shop, maybe one people don't think about."

"Along with making clothes that always fit."

She nodded, then tilted her head. "Yes, but not in the way you might mean."

"Oh?"

"The shop has made me a better seamstress. Where I'm from, women always learn to sew well, though. 'Womanly duties.'" She rolled her eyes. "But the key to making something fit is being able to *measure* it. To understand exactly what *will* fit, and exactly *how* it'll fit. That's what the shop really does."

"I suspect," Sam said slowly, "you mean more than you're saying."

Prudence smiled. "I knew the first time I saw you that you *fit* here. The measure of you—the pub is what fits you. And. . ." she flushed a bit here, and looked away, "you know. Everything."

"Actually," Sam said somewhat wearily, "I *don't* know. What else do I 'fit?'"

Prudence was in a full blush now, her skin tinged a deep red. "It's not for me to say," she mumbled.

Sam sighed. "Fine, fine. More mysteries of the village. I like it, it keeps things interesting. So that," she continued, nodding to the spread-out orc skin. "What's the plan?"

"Oh," Prudence said, grinning and turning back to the table. "You'll see. I may need some help, though. I didn't think it'd be this heavy."

————

The metal armature that Warren had built was heavier than Sam expected, and combined with the weight of the cast-off orc skin it was almost too much to carry. Fortunately, Warren was able to support most of its weight, and merely needed help guiding it across the road, through the pub into the back alley, through the grocery, and out into the village square.

All three pegasi looked up as they struggled to get the thing through the door, off the walkway, and into the grass. The mares began flicking their wings nervously.

"I don't think we should put it in the main gateway," Jen had mused when she'd examined the completed structure in the smithy. "We don't know how much takeoff space those things need, and if we box them into the green, they could do some damage."

Cole had been summoned, and he and his family had hurriedly cleared a pathway through the grocery's back and front rooms, all the way to its front door. The pub had been the tricky bit, since the entire structure had to be passed *over* the bar, then turned sideways to fit through the back door.

With Jen and Sam steadying the thing, Warren lifted it halfway over his head and then drove it down hard, sinking its base pole half an arm's length into the soft earth. All three of them quickly retreated to the walkway, unconsciously covering their noses and mouths with a hand to help block the growing stench.

The pegasi were not amused.

"We used to have terrible problems with crows," Prudence

had explained last night as Sam helped her tug the orc skin into positions so she could stitch it back together. "And so some of the men would take old clothes, stuff them with straw, and hang them on a wooden cross of sorts. They called them 'scarecrows.' So I thought maybe, if the skin alone wasn't going to do it, this would help."

"This" was an iron framework in a half-hunched position, over which the orc's skin was draped. Straw had been brought in from the stable next door to fill the thing out, and they were left with a creditable figure that Prudence called a *scarepegasi.* All that was missing was a head, but Prudence was deft with her heavy scissors and leather-sewing kit, and she fashioned a reasonable facsimile from some of the thing's back skin. Carved tree branches stood in for the fearsome tusks, and black glass beads were glued in for the eyes.

The stallion shrieked a warning, and the two mares fled, their wings already spread. The three pegasi cantered out the main gate, turned east onto the trade road, and were airborn before they'd cleared the east gate.

"Well," Jen said, placing her hands on her hips. "Guess that worked."

"The book suggests we'll have to keep moving it around a few times a day for the next sennight," Vamir said, stepping down from the walkway where he'd been watching the proceedings. "Warren, as heavy as that looks, I'm afraid it'll be on you."

"Small price to pay," the smith said with a wide smile. "I'll start now." He heaved the scarepegasi out of the ground, moved it toward the center of the square, and then shoved it back into the earth. He panted a bit as he stood. "Didn't realize the skin itself would weigh so much. That thing must have been fearsome."

"That doesn't do it justice," Sam snorted. The mental prodding she'd been feeling all morning was becoming more insistent. "We're expecting today," she said.

"Yeah, I've been getting it too," Jen agreed. "Go on, open the pub. Let's see what the day has to bring. Everyone!" she called more loudly. All of the villagers, including the kids, had turned out to see if the scarepegasi would work. "Kids, I know you won't love this, but let's start getting buckets of water and dumping them on all this dung. See if we can't start washing it away. It'll make a muddy mess for a while, but the grass grows quickly. Start from the center and work your way out. The faster we can get rid of this smell, the better."

This was met with a few desultory groans, but from their pleased expressions Sam could tell the kids—especially the old ones who'd born the brunt of the mucking—were pleased to see the end of the flying pests.

Sam took the alley back to the pub, and started wiping down tables. The door opened, and Calder poked his head through. "Morning, Calder. Come on in. Surprised you're not out on the lake already."

He shook his head. "Signs were wrong this morning. Got the kids neatening up the shop. What I wanted to ask you about, actually."

Sam raised an eyebrow. "The shop?"

"The kids," Calder corrected. "Specifically Bryn."

Now Sam frowned. "What's wrong with him?"

"Nothing's *wrong*. Just. . . the lake's not for him. Or he's not for the lake, one or t'other. He's game enough, but his head's not in it. Won't force a trade on him like m'father did me. Was wondering if you might could use a set of hands 'round this place. I know the pub won't. . . you know. With him. But he can fetch and carry, and he's a bright boy."

Now both of Sam's eyebrows rose in surprise. "I. . . you know, I'll take you up on that. For as long as *he* wants to, at least. I could use the help, especially on busy days, bussing tables and running for food and the like." She listened for a moment to see if the pub objected, but it remained silent. "Nothing tells me the pub doesn't approve, so yes. Happy to have him."

Calder's expression was one of immense relief, and Sam

wondered how long this had been bothering him. "I'll send him over straight away, and thank you."

"Of course, Calder. I'm the one who should be thanking you!"

"Just happy to have the boy. . . happy."

"We'll get along great."

Calder nodded and ducked out while Sam continued preparing the pub for the day's custom. The pub's prodding hadn't been *deeply* urgent, and she didn't get the sense that they'd be looking at anything dire that day but. . . there was something in the air. Something unusual.

Maybe, Sam thought brightly, *today will be the day we find our other two!*

eighteen

. . .

THE REST OF THE MORNING, and all of the afternoon, passed as a blessedly "business as usual" day. Travelers began trickling in around midmorning, most of those stopping for a bite and a quick chat before moving on.

Treasure seekers. "Honestly, there are more than a few orc hunters already up this way." *Compass.* "You know, you should stop by Mistral Adventures, just inside the west gate. Down the trade road and on your right. Ask the proprietor about a compass. Oh, I'm sure you do, but trust me."

Heroic quest. "Dragons? Really? Huh, who knew. No, I've never heard so much as a rumor of a suggestion they even exist anymore, let alone in the Mistrals. Aren't they cold-blooded? No? Well, best of luck to you." *South.* "You know, this sounds crazy but. . . do they have lake-dragons? Yeah? Again, not that I've heard anything, but. . . maybe head south instead? No, not here, but the next village to the west does fishing excursions, maybe they'd be willing to rent you a boat?"

"Heyla, Sam, how goes it?" Minnie asked, bustling through from the back. "I'm almost out of stew and wondered if I should put something else on?"

"I'd say so," Sam said, gauging her feelings. "Should get a

break for a couple of candlemarks, and then we'll start getting the evening crowd. How're you fixed for rooms?"

"Empty, at the moment, so bring them on. Hmm. You know, Calder dropped off some fish I need to use up. Maybe I'll make a chowder. Let me go see if Cole has any leek."

"Sounds great."

Knows where they're going with a hint of heroic quest. "Did you say 'rabbits?' You're just. . . hunting rabbits? I mean. . . all over the place, really. The lower foothills, especially. Um, we're almost out of stew, let me see what's left. Minnie's making a fish chowder next, if you don't mind—no? Okay, be right back. Do you want a couple of ales, first? Copper for two? Coming right up." *Weirdos,* Sam thought. "Hey, Bryn, mind stepping in and bringing back whatever stew Minnie's still got in the pot?"

Calder's eldest had been a godsend, especially on a busy day like this. It seemed Sam couldn't get herself out from behind the bar, and so the tall, lanky boy had been running bowls of stew, fresh steins of ale, and hunks of cheese and bread all day. He'd been to the dryads' *twice* already for fresh wheels, and Makota had been forced to put another batch of heart brown bread into the oven after both she and Minnie ran out before noon. The baker had sent *her* oldest with trays of pastries, which Bryn had been enthusiastically talking up to customers all morning. The boy was a natural salesperson, Sam thought cheerfully. Everyone with something edible to sell was going to do *really* well from now on.

Heroic quest. "A *volcano?* Four hells, no. The Mistrals aren't volcanic. No, you're on the wrong end of the continent—you want the Flameheight range, all along the western sea. No, no idea why anyone sent you this way. No, I swear, not a volcano to be seen in the Mistrals. They wouldn't be so damned cold! Why do you need a vol—just a ring? You know, we've a smithy across the road, he could probably—no? Ah, magical. Sorry. Yes, the inn next door is excellent, highly recommended and Minnie puts on an amazing breakfast. Just ring the bell as you go in, she'll probably be in the kitchen." *The things people get up to in the south,* Sam thought with mild amusement. *Magic rings that have to be thrown in volcanos.*

Darby poked his head in the front door. "Big group coming through, Sam! Dad says they look like mercs!" Sam's eyes widened in alarm until Darby continued. "But he says they look like they're just off a job and passing through!"

"Bryn, go run for more cheese and bread. Go the back way—pop in and tell Minnie we've got a crowd coming through. Quick as you can!" Then, as a conservatively attired couple stepped warily into the pub, "Greetings, travelers! Welcome to the Broken Claw! How may I serve?"

"Just a bite of something simple, if you can spare it. And two mugs of small beer, if you have it," the man said in a low voice that seemed designed to take up as little space as possible.

"Easily done," Sam said cheerfully. "Two coppers total, if fish chowder suits. If not, I'll have some bread and cheese here in a moment or two." Her eyes flicked up, and she raised an eyebrow as the ball seemed to waver between *Personal reasons* and *Heroic quest. That's an odd combination,* she thought and she stepped in the back to pour the beers.

"Bread and cheese will be fine," the man said as he and his—wife?—settled onto a bench.

"Bryn should be back in a tic and we'll get you served. It'll be hot and fresh from the oven, to boot. Say, where are you headed today? We try to keep tabs on road conditions and such."

"We came in from the west," the woman said quietly, "and we're heading east."

No, the pub suddenly insisted. *Danger.*

"We, ah—there've been some reports of danger out east. Bandits and the like. Might want to consider putting up the night, or even—"

The man was shaking his head. "We cannot," he insisted in the same quiet voice. "The gods have called us east."

"There were portents," the woman said.

"And we must be off urgently, only stopping long enough to sustain ourselves."

Sam felt the pub consider this, and could amost sense it sorting through options. *Cloaks,* it whispered.

"Well. . . then at least let me suggest you head back to just inside our west gate. Mistral Adventures. See Tyran for cloaks— he'll part with them for a very reasonable price, I assure you, but the nights are still chill here, and you're not dressed for them."

The couple exchanged glances, and the man reluctantly nodded. "Last night was. . . quite bitter," he admitted. "Thank you. We shall do as you suggest."

Sam hoped the cloaks they eventually bought would lend them some protection, or make them less noticable on the road. Whatever problem the pub was concerned about, its gift would hopefully mitigate the risk. "Ah, here's Bryn with the bread and cheese. Over here, Bryn," she called to the boy. "Cut them a good portion."

She turned toward the door as a dozen or so horses trotted to a halt just outside. Darby was already running up to speak to the riders. *These'll be the mercs,* Sam thought with interest, pulling several steins from under the bar. *Let's see how this goes.*

———

The mercs were indeed coming off a job, all dozen of them cheerful and tired with plenty of silver and copper in their purses. They ate through all of Minnie's fish chowder, proclaiming it the best they'd had in many moons, and got Sam well into a fresh barrel of ale before they called it quits. "Is there any chance," their leader asked Sam, "of rooms for the night? We could probably get a great deal further with the light we've left, but to be honest. . ."

"To be honest, we've earned a quiet night of food and ale, and yours is the best we've had along this road," another merc said with a laugh.

"Minnie owns the Weary Head just next door," Sam chuckled. "It'll be a squeeze, but if you're willing to go two to a room, maybe three in the large room downstairs, she should be able to fit you all. I think you'll be her second custom today, unless someone's gone in without coming here first." The pub was muttering something she couldn't make out. It seemed unsettled, but not sure what to do about it. "And you're welcome to stay and eat and drink once you've arranged for rooms," she added. *Maybe it needs more time to study them.* The ball over the door was drifting lazily in a circle, giving her nothing useful to go on.

"Costa, you go arrange for the rooms," the leader nodded to one of the shorter men. "We'll just stay here! Is there any more of that excellent bread?"

Bryn stepped up. "Aye, sir. And if you've a taste for something sweet, our baker's promised a tray of apple tarts in half a 'mark or so."

"Done!" the mercs roared as one, slapping copper coins on their tables.

Minnie poked her head in from the back. "Sam, how're we— oh, goodness," she said, catching sight of the crowd in the pub.

"They'll be renting you out for the night, Minnie, so head back over. And they're hungry, so whatever you want to cook up, I'm sure it'll be well-received."

"For this lot, I'll send Trevor to the storehouse for a joint." She raised her voice. "You lot okay with roast venison?"

Another roar of approval sent her on her way.

The minstrel stepped in from his break, his face lighting up as he saw the crowd. He quickly resumed his place in the corner and struck up a bawdy tavern song. The mercs cheered, tossed coins at him, and raised their voices to sing along.

The constable stepped in after a minute, and smiled at the good-natured goings-on. "It's nice to see the place like this," she said, pulling Sam to one side and speaking as softly as possible, given the din.

"It is," Sam said, watching the mercs goad the minstrel into another bawdy song. She felt something, and turned to see Jen staring intently at her. "What?"

"You're. . . you *do* feel like you fit, don't you? Here, I mean?"

"Oh, I do," Sam said, turning back to the crowd.

"You haven't let up on that sword since I walked in," Jen pointed out.

Sam started, looked down, and realized she'd been gently brushing Nailbiter's hilt. "Huh."

"Anything you'd like to share?"

Sam looked back at the mercs.

> *In the tavern's den, where the ale flows free,*
> *Wenches wink and jest, for a golden fee.*
> *The minstrel strums, with a cheeky grin,*
> *Raucous laughter for the ones who win.*

"You miss it, don't you?" Jen said, leaning in so she could speak more softly.

Sam nodded slowly. "Some of it, I guess." She snorted. "Not the rough camping, *not* the terrible food, *definitely not* the endless patrols, *absolutely not* the battles." She paused. "Mostly not the battles."

"Orc hunt revived something, maybe?"

Another slow nod. "Maybe." She considered. "Maybe not. I know the adrenaline rush used to be. . . you know. Everything. Up there, it was just *terror*. I truly thought we'd be killed."

"So not that."

"No. Not that."

Jen as quiet for a moment. "Did you ever find love, in all those years in the companies?"

Sam shrugged. "I mean, you do. Here and there, right? A toss in the cot. Makes you feel alive again."

Jen shook her head. "No, not *lust*. Not even. . . comfort, if you want to call it that. Love."

Sam turned and met the constable's eyes. They looked a lot like her own, she knew: leathery at the corners, flinty colors. Hard. Eyes that had seen too much, and lived to tell about it. "Once, I think."

"The shieldmate you spoke of?"

Sam nodded. "Leeta."

"Could be that's what you're looking for?"

Sam turned back to the mercs.

> *Amidst the merriment, where the jesters prance,*
> *Wenches dance on tables, in a wild romance.*
> *The minstrel's song, with a lewd refrain,*
> *Bottoms up! for the merry and the sane.*

Something tugged at Sam's heart, and she knew it wasn't the mercs themselves, or the life they led. It wasn't the fighting, it wasn't even the money—she'd been paid well, but what did you spend it on? Ale, cheap food, maybe a night in the arms of someone you'd paid to care for you? No, it wasn't that. "Could be," she sighed.

"You've. . . *felt* it here, haven't you?"

Sam turned back to Jen. "Felt what?"

"Against those pegasi. Even when we ran off those thugs. You felt. . . *it.*"

A deep awareness started to spread through Sam's chest. "That. . . *feeling.*"

"Like a click."

"Yeah."

Jen sighed. "Look, I'm no good at this kind of thing. But we're two old battle axes. We both know we *fit* here. Gods know the village isn't coy about that. Even Prudence sees it."

Prudence? Sam thought. Then her eyes widened as awareness evolved into understanding. *Not my story to tell,* she'd said.

"And you and I. . . we have it. *We* fit as well. I felt the click."

"I did too," Sam said softly.

"Think we could. . . keep it?" Jen asked, her eyes softening at the edges, their hard glint easing.

"I do," Sam said simply. "I—" she frowned and leaned to see past Jen out the front door. Two horses slowed from a gallop to a stop. They were foamed and weary, their heads hanging low and their coats covered in dust. Their riders dismounted and headed directly for the pub.

As one, Jen and Sam turned and stepped out to meet them on the walkway.

"Bandits!" they panted. "Please, you have to give us shelter! It's a huge company of them!"

Jen took a deep breath. "Well. It's come."

The pub suddenly felt. . . *Is it anxious?* Sam asked herself. *Or is that. . . anticipation?*

Bartender and constable turned as a *large* number of horses trotted through the east gate. Ellis, the man who'd led the group Leota had driven off days before, was riding three or four back, and he frowned as he spotted the two women. At the front of the group, riding a tall, heavily built horse, was a man dressed in simple, battered riding leathers, a worn burgundy cloak thrown over one shoulder. His shaggy salt-and-pepper hair was full of road dust, and the sword sheath at his waist looked worn but well cared-for. "Ladies," he said in a gruff, gravelly voice as his horse clopped to a front before them. "My name is Cragg. I presume you're the ones I need to speak to?"

"About what?" Jen asked, her own raspy voice guarded.

His eyes swept the trade road, taking in the buildings to either side, and the tall wall that enclosed part of the square. "About my new village."

nineteen

. . .

THE LEADER OF THE MERCS, along with a couple of his fighters, had stepped out of the pub behind Jen and Sam. "Trouble here?" the leader asked quietly.

Jen was staring at the newcomers, and Sam realized she wasn't staring at the men on horseback. Instead, she was focused on a group of people on foot, who'd been brought up at the rear of the group. "Who're they?" Sam asked, pointing.

Cragg turned. "Ah. Some folks we came across on the road," he said easily. "They'll be helping. . . populate my new village."

Sam counted seven miserable-looking people, their clothes covered in road dust. One man had a furball of some kind perched on one shoulder, putting Sam in mind of the creature she'd seen in the Mistrals. "Horseshit," she declared, reaching for her weapon. "There's no—"

"Hold," Jen said quietly, laying a hand on Sam's forearm. "We're not. . . this isn't a battle we win."

"Wise," Cragg said, turning back to them.

"We've got your back," the merc leader said quietly behind them.

"No," Jen said, shaking her head slowly. "No, I won't have this become a battleground. That isn't what this place is for. It's not who we are. Please," she added, turning to the mercs, "go back inside."

"You can't—" Sam hissed.

"No," Jen repeated, gripping Sam's forearm tightly before letting it go. "Okay, Cragg. Tell us how this is going to work."

Cragg nodded and slid out of his saddle. He stepped onto the walkway in front of the two women. He kept his voice low. "We'll set up a toll on the road," he began. "And there'll be a tax on your businesses. Everything you take in. Five percent, nothing too onerous. In exchange, we'll guard the road. Keep out any. . . bad elements." He gave them a tired grin, clearly aware of the irony of that statement.

"We can trust your men?" Jen asked. "I won't have any. . . behavior."

Cragg nodded. "You can. I'll be honest, ladies. We're. . . tired. Tired of the road life. Tired of—"

"You were chased out of Gray Foal Pass, weren't you?" Sam asked in a hard voice. "Maybe by a couple of Rangers?"

Cragg raised an eyebrow, but nodded. "Aye. By *one* Ranger. Got the villagers who hadn't fled on his side."

"What makes you think that won't happen here?"

"Ah. Your little village is much more defensible. Practically a fortress. Surprised you haven't set up better defenses, actually. And. . . not to put too fine a point upon it, but you'll all be staying. Walls that keep people out also keep them in."

"So we're to be slaves?" Sam spat. Jen laid another warning hand on her forearm.

"Not at all," Cragg said, shaking his head. "Truly. You're free to run your businesses, so long as you pay the tax. But I won't have the place emptied out."

"We've a witch," Sam said.

"Sam," Jen said urgently, squeezing her arm again.

"No, it's fine. I'm aware." He grinned slightly. "Ellis was. . . very clear." He tapped his chest, and Sam realized he was wearing one of the intricately inscribed metal badges his first thugs had worn. "I've taken care to guard against that kind of thing, this time. I've no problem with witches and wizards, if they keep their place." His tone made it clear that ones who didn't would be dealt with harshly.

"Toll. Tax. What else?" Jen asked as Sam opened her mouth to say something.

Cragg shrugged. "Housing. A barracks situation is fine for the men. I'll want a place of my own."

"Like a mayor, then?" Jen asked.

Cragg shrugged again. "If you like."

"Food?"

"Obviously, but credited toward your tax."

Jen jerked her chin at the prisoners. "And them?"

Cragg turned again to survey the ragged-looking group. "They'll be staying. We'll need somewhere to. . . keep them. Until they. . . acclimate. I'm told you have a gaol."

Jen nodded slowly. "It's too small, but we have an empty shop that they'll fit into. For the time being."

"For the time being," Cragg agreed. He raised his voice. "Close the road gates, men. No traffic through, today." Four men dismounted and ran to comply. "You're making a wise choice, constable."

"Mmm. Sam, why don't you ask the men in the pub to head to the inn for the—"

"Actually, we'll be on our way," the merc leader said coldly. "I'm assuming you" have no problem with that?" he added to Cragg in a menacing tone.

"None at all. Let the mercs and their horses out before you bar the gates!" he called.

"Then Sam, why don't you show our new leaders to the pub," Jen said.

"Actually, we'll—" Cragg began.

Jen shook her head. "You'll have no trouble from us, but it's going to take a few hours to clear out some of the empty homes. We'll get all the kids to help out. Why don't you just relax in the meantime? We'll get some food into you, and see to your horses."

Cragg's eyes narrowed. "No tricks."

Jen shook her head. "No tricks. Post guards, if you want. Sam and Bryn will take a bite of everything you're served, if you want."

"I will—" Sam started with some heat.

"Peace, Sam," Jen snapped.

"If you hate us after a sennight," Cragg told Sam, "you can go. We mean to make this a home, not a prison."

Sam stared daggers at him. "You have a strange way of making a start of it," she said coldly. "Pub's this way."

The mercs were already filing out, shooting cold looks at the newcomers as they made their way to the stable yard. They took only a few moments to saddle up and leave the town. Their leader was the last out, and the look he shot at Sam left little doubt about what a stupid decision he thought this was.

Half of Cragg's men, along with their leader, stepped into the pub. As Sam followed them, Jen was already leading the prisoners to the main gates, followed by two of Cragg's men. Jen was whispering something to one of the prisoners. Sam frowned, wondering what the constable was saying. *Probably telling them to be good little prisoners,* she thought with some heat. *Lie down and take it.* Sam knew she couldn't fight this many men on her own. *But between us, she and I could* have. *I don't understand.*

Minnie was waiting behind the bar, her face a mask of fear and confusion. "Chowder for everyone, Minnie," Sam ordered. "Bryn will help you carry." The boy's expression was all fear. "And if you're getting low, I'd put some more on. Bryn, how're we fixed for bread?" The boy looked to the bar, where several fresh loaves were cooling. "Perfect." Sam forced her tone to something resembling neutrality, because she knew she couldn't manage cheer at this point. "I'll cut it up. Go, both of you."

They vanished through the door behind the bar.

"Ale, gentlemen?" Sam asked. "We've small beer and wine,

as well. I'd. . . let's stay away from anything stronger for now, if you please."

"Agreed," Cragg said in a tone that brooked no dissent. His men shrugged and sat as Sam cleared the merc's steins and carried them behind the bar.

A few minutes later, Vamir stepped into the pub. One of the thugs half-rose, but Sam waved him down. "He runs the book-shop, he's no fighter," she said. "Vamir, what are you doing here?"

He proferred a stack of clean sheets of paper and a couple of graphite stencils. "Jen sent me," he said quietly. "She said these men might want to start drafting out their tax tables. I had a suggestion along those lines," he added, scanning the group in an effort to identify the leader.

"Suggestions?" Cragg asked.

Vamir met the man's gaze. "Just suggestions. Most of our business is in foodstuffs, but equipment from the outfitter's normally goes for higher prices. A flat tax might not be the best for the overall revenue picture, if you take my meaning."

Cragg's eyebrows rose. "I see. Why don't you join us and explain your. . . suggestions."

"Of course."

Heat rose in Sam's heart, and she clenched her jaw as Vamir sat and began quietly conferring with Cragg. She forced herself to continue filling steins, making a show of sipping from each one as she set them on the bar. Bryn returned a moment later, his arms balancing a half-dozen bowls of fish chowder, which he began passing out. "Take a taste from each one, Bryn," Sam instructed. The boy stared at her for a moment before nodding and complying. She carried the steins in pairs, sitting them at the end of each table and letting the men pass them along.

The tension in the pub was so thick Sam thought she could see it. In her mind, the pub was muttering something—but when she took a moment to pay attention to it, absentmindedly contin-uing to fill steins of ale, it didn't seem. . . *angry.* Confused, maybe. *No, that's not it either,* she said, trying to tune out the atmosphere in the pub and focus on what it was feeling. *It's. . . content? How is that even possible?* Is this what it felt it was missing? A *mayor?* Couldn't it even read these men? Didn't it even care—she caught herself as the stein she was holding overflowed, covering her hand in ale. She shook herself and carried another pair to the tables.

The eyes of every man in the room, save for Cragg and Vamir, followed her warily. She ignored them, her eyes flicking to the device over the pub's door. The ball was lazily rolling through *Personal matters* and *Heroic quest,* although it was spending more time in the former section. *What in the four hells. . .?* she asked herself. The pub continued muttering incoherently in the back of her mind, but she was getting a definite sense of. . . *It feels settled,* she decided, shaking her head in silent confusion.

"So you see," Vamir was saying quietly, "some of the more luxury goods, the teas, even some of the fresh produce, could sustain a six or even seven percent tax, but on the essentials—dried meats, cheeses, basic provisions—a four percent would be more bearable. But for a room tax—Minnie only charges a copper, and you could honestly go to two through most of the season, and four if you included dinners as well as breakfasts. If you add that up, you actually come out with an average that's higher than five percent, in total."

"Mmm," Cragg mused.

This is insanity, Sam thought in angry bewilderment. *This can't be how this ends, with this thug and his men. . . if a* single Ranger *ran them out of Gray Foal Pass, why can't we—*

"Cragg!"

It was Jen's voice, shouting from outside. Except. . . Sam frowned. All her easy compliance was gone from that single call. The cold iron Sam was used to hearing was back.

Cragg heard it too. "Everyone with me," he said quickly, rising and striding out the door.

Sam followed the last of the invaders. They'd spread out just off the walkway, and Sam remained in the pub's door. She waved a hand behind her, indicating that Bryn and Vamir should stay inside. That same hand fell to rest on Nailbiter's hilt. At the same time, the pub seemed to *sigh* in her mind. Her sense of it was suddenly sharper and clearer than it had ever been, as if she —or maybe it—had shaken off some kind of haze, or woken from a half-dream.

"Change in plans, Cragg," Jen said flatly. Her right arm was held slightly away from her body, and Sam recognized that she was preparing to summon her weapon. "We've decided we don't need a mayor. Or your protection. Time to move on."

Cragg stepped forward, shaking his head. "Are you mad, woman? Even with your magic weapon, I—"

"I won't need it," Jen said firmly. "You've come in peace. So to speak. You've stayed in peace, as it were. But you've made it clear you intend to control entry and exit to and from the village, correct? With your toll?"

Cragg nodded warily.

"That's unacceptable to us, I'm afraid. So I'll ask you one time: Will you leave in peace?"

"I don't want to spill your blood, woman," Cragg said roughly, although Sam thought she could actually detect some regret in his voice, "but we won't be leaving."

"You heard him," Jen said loudly.

Who's she talking—

Sam's eyebrows rose as the village began to. . . *rumble.*

Cragg's men drew their swords.

"You've shown your inclination toward violence," Jen intoned.

Sam's head whipped to her right as a heavy wooden *slam* echoed through the road. She realized the village's main gates had closed. The two men who'd followed the prisoners in were standing just outside those gates, looking confused. They began pushing at the gates, but they couldn't budge them.

The "prisoners" were nowhere to be seen.

The rumbling was increasing both in volume and intensity.

Gods above and below, Sam thought as she realized what was happening. *The gate turrets are crumbling!*

And so they were: the tall stone turrets that bracketed both the west and east road gates were falling stone by stone. Cragg's men backed quickly away as the heavy stones fell. No longer supported, the thick gates themselves fell inward, *thudding* to the ground and raising two huge clouds of dust at either end of the village. The gates seemed to shatter then, the individual planks separating and rattling to the ground.

Gods of mercy. . . Sam thought as the dust began to clear.

The stones of the turrets and the planks of the gates had begun to *reassemble themselves.* But not into their previous form.

As Sam watched, her jaw agape, the stones were rolling toward each other, rolling themselves *atop* each other. In just an eyeblink, the stones at either end of the road had formed two short, stout pillars. . . which then merged into one thicker pillar. . .

They're golems, Sam realized.

Two enormous stone figures rose from the dusty road. The gate's planks had formed themselves into two crude swords and two heavy shields, and the golems—easily three times Sam's height—wielded them with a quiet grace. The huge figures moved with a grinding of stone against stone, adopting a fighting stance, "swords" raised in an *en garde* position, their tall shields positioned to cover most of their bodies.

"Four hells," Cragg whispered.

"Go, Cragg," Jen ordered. "Go, and take your men with you. Never return. This is what awaits you, if you do. We don't judge you or your destiny, but neither of them has a place here."

The men's horses were already stomping nervously, milling against one another and knocking their riders aside as they tried to cluster in the exact middle of the trade road—as far as possible from the menacing stone guardians.

"Magic. . ." Cragg breathed as he stared at the western golem. One hand touched the metal badge on his chest.

"That won't protect you," Jen said wryly. "Saddle up. Get—"

A vision crashed into Sam's brain. *The Qilin, fire streaming up from its eyes, sparks scattering with its breath. Marking the passing of a great leader. . . or the rise of one.*

"Cragg!" Sam shouted. The man's head snapped to her. "Why?"

He frowned. "Why what?"

"Why. . . here? Why Gray Foal Pass?"

His frown deepened. "I told you. We're tired of life on the road. We mean to make a home."

"But you can't do that by *taking* someone else's."

He stared at her for a moment, and then shrugged. "It's all we know. We can't start from scratch." His men, desperately trying to grab their horses' reins, ignored the conversation. The giant stone creatures stood absolutely still, waiting for. . . something.

"I think. . ." Sam said, trying to understand everything that was washing through her mind, "I think you're meant—"

Yes, the pub said, its hundred muddled whispers finally coalescing into one.

"—to be a leader," Sam finished, her voice gaining confidence. "Maybe even a great one. But not," she added, shaking her head, "here. We don't need a leader, here. That's not what this place is."

Another vision swept through her. "I came in from the west. A day's hard ride from here, off the trade road, there's what's left of a village. A few good, stone buildings. Plenty of trees to make more. A huge field behind it—you're further from the foothills."

Seed, the pub whispered.

Sam blinked.

"Sam!"

She turned to see Tyran running toward her, a leather bag in one hand. He eased past the mass of horses, eyeing them warily, and handed the bag to Sam.

"Take this," she said, holding it out to Cragg. Something had come over him, and he walked over to her as if in a dream, sheathing his sword. He took the bag and blinked at it. "It's a seed," Sam said.

"For. . . crops?"

A dozen more murmurs filled Sam's mind. "Yes," she said, shaking her head as she tried to sort it out. "And more. It's the seed. . . of a village. That's your destiny, I think. It'll be work," she added. "Hard work. You can't just *take*. But if you're serious, if you want to settle and have a home. . . that's your start."

His eyes seeemed locked on the leather bag.

"Don't open it until you're there," she added.

He nodded slowly and looked up at her. His head turned back and forth as he took in the enormous stone warriors, and the mass of horses his men were finally managing to sort out. Then he turned back to her, and nodded again. "Saddle up," he said. His tone was quiet, but it carried a surety, an authority, that Sam hadn't heard before. His command carried clearly down the road, echoing low from the golems' shields despite its softness.

His men needed no encouragement, vaulting themselves in their saddles. One of them led Cragg's horse to him. He seemed to consider it for a moment, and then looped the leather bag's ties over his head and across one shoulder before mounting. He met Sam's eyes once more, and Sam thought he looked less haggard, less worn than when he'd rode in.

As if responding to some silent command, the west golem, stone grinding against stone, pivoted on one heel and took a half-step back, placing its back toward the stable yard and leaving a clear path out of the village.

Cragg kicked his horse, and it leaped forward into a gallop. His men's horses needed no further encouragement, moving from walk to trot to canter to gallop before they'd reached the golem.

"Well," Jen said quietly as the dust settled behind them.

The golems began to move.

"This'll be a bit loud," Jen warned.

The two stone creatures stood upright, the west one turning so it once agains stood in the middle of the trade road, facing inward.

Then they collapsed.

Their heavy stone blocks tumbled to the road, raising two more clouds of thick dust. Their swords and shields fell apart as well, once again individual planks falling loosely to the earth. Almost immediately, stone and wood began shifting and rolling, and within a hundred heartbeats, as the dust began to settle once more, two tall, wooden gates swung open, supported by stone turrets.

"What," Sam asked quietly when the air had cleared, "happened?"

"The icosagon," Leota's voice rang out. Sam turned to see that the village gates had already swung open. Leota was walking slowly toward the pub, supported by Cole.

Sam shook her head. "Gonna need some help."

"The prisoners," Jen said with a wide smile. "That one man with the ink-stained fingers? He's the proprietor of our new mapmaker's shop. And the one with that little puffball on his shoulder? He runs our new exotic menagerie. I expect we'll have critters storming down from the Mistrals any minute now, looking to take up residence."

"Map—what?" Sam asked, her mind whirling with confusion.

"The village needed two more people to settle here and run shops. Shops that can serve travelers, and a mapmaker and seller of magical, exotic familiars are a perfect fit," Leota explained, stepping onto the walkway next to Sam. "That *completed* it."

"Didn't expect your little performance," Jen said, "but when I saw those two I figured, if I could convince them—wasn't hard

—and get them into empty shops, then the village would defend itself."

"With some direction," Leota smiled wearily. "And I'm going to nap for a moon, trust me."

Indeed, in Sam's mind, what had once been a quiet, sleepy presence was now a sharp, alert, querying. . . well, still a *presence,* but much more *present.* It was the pub, and it already felt more coherent and engaged than she'd become used to.

"That bit with the abandoned village. . ." Jen said, a question in her tone.

"Real," Sam said, blinking her way back to the moment. "It *is* his destiny. Their destinies. Whatever. That bag. . ."

"Practically shoved itself into my hand," Tyran agreed. "Felt like the shop all but physically pushed me into the road with it."

"So that's it," Cole said. "Right? We're safe now?"

Jen nodded slowly. "I believe we—"

"Look!" Tyran exclaimed, pointing to the sky.

twenty

. . .

EVERYONE SKIDDED to a stop at the main gates, their heads craned back at the three. . . four. . . *Curse it, there's* five *of them,* Sam thought furiously as the flying shapes—unmistakably pegasi—circled.

"Everyone stay back!" Jen shouted. Sam's lowered her eyes and realized nearly the whole village had turned out, with a few of them stepping into the grass so that they could see upwards. "Back on the walkway! Kids inside! Vamir, I thought they'd be gone for good," she added more quietly as the old elf finally joined them.

"The book wasn't clear," he said uncertainly. "It just said they hated orcs."

"They left fast enough when we put it out," Warren said. "I was about to go move it again."

"I think you're going to want to stay out," Sam said. "Look, they're coming in for a landing."

It happened so fast it made Sam's head spin: the five pegasi descended, cantering in a circle aroud the village green to shed momentum, and then turning to the scarepegasi, which was still posted near the trees in the center of the green. As one, the five beasts attacked, slashing at the orc skin with their sharp hooves and gnashing at it with their teeth, their wings spread and over-lapping each others'. In moments, the "orc" was nothing but tatters, and even the iron frame had been beaten and twisted out of shape.

The pegasi snorted with satisfaction, lowering their wings and slowly backing away. After a few moments' lack of retaliation from the "orc," they shook themselves and began wandering in different directions, their heads lowered to munch the grass. One of them looked up at the crowd standing at the main gate, huffed in either annoyance or arrogance, and lifted its tail to deposit an especially slimy-looking load.

"Four mares," Leota said quietly as a sense of depression settled over the watching villagers.

"Nothing is going to get rid of them," Sam moaned.

Just then, a door next to Prudence's shop slammed open and two small, gray-furred. . . *somethings* darted out. They made a beeline for the nearest pegasus, which lifted its head and backed away in alarm as the two critters began hissing and yapping at it. It looked at its nearest companion, and its body language is clear: *What are these, and what do I do with them?*

"What are those?" Sam asked.

"They. . . *look* like meowolf cubs," Vamir said hesitantly. "I've not known them to be so. . . aggressive."

"They're going to get stomped," Warren observed. He wasn't wrong: the male pegasus had joined the female that the two little furballs were yapping at. Fresh off their "victory" with the scarepegasi, the pegasi began snorting and pawing the ground, lowering their heads at their diminutive attackers and raising their wings from their flanks.

A man came hurrying out of the open door, and Sam recognized him as one of the former prisoners. "Stop it, you two!" he shouted.

"Stay on the walkway!" Jen ordered.

The man pulled up just shy of the walkway's edge as the two pegasi raised their heads and huffed a warning, their ears flat to their heads. The other three mares turned and began rustling their wings in agitation.

"Get back here!" the man ordered the two cubs.

"He didn't come in with those, did he?" Sam asked softly. "I mean, it was less than an hour ago."

"It's a complete menagerie now," Jen replied. "Wouldn't surprise me if he had a dozen more exotic critters in there already. The village moves fast."

"Wow."

"You know," Leota said very softly, her eyes unfocused, "it feels them, now."

Jen frowned. "The cubs?"

The cubs were, in fact, responding to the new shop owner, backing away from the annoyed pegasi and onto the walkway. They'd stopped yapping, but were still hissing angrily.

"No," Leota said. "The pegasi. Before, the village didn't even seem to know they existed. I could sense it feeding magic into the green to regrow the grass, but it didn't have any reaction to the pegasi themselves. Now. . . it's aware of them."

"Does that mean we can. . . do something about them?" Sam asked slowly.

"No, it's worse than that," Jen grumbled. "Serve all, remember?"

Sam blinked. "I mean, they hardly 'came in peace.'"

She felt the *click* as Jen's mind fell into sync with hers. "No, they did not," the constable murmured, tilting her head and looking at the pegasi. They'd given one final snort at the shop owner and gone back to grazing. For his part, the man had gathered the two cubs into his arms and was backing into his shop, his eyes nervously locked on the flying beasts.

"Was there anything else in the book?" Jen asked.

Vamir shook his head. "Nothing we'd be able to try, no."

"What? Are we short a virgin?" Sam asked, half-joking.

"That's unicorns," Vamir said seriously. "But no, I'm sure some of the—"

"Enough," Jen said firmly. She squared her shoulders and set off onto the green, stalking quickly toward the stallion.

The pegasi barely had time to get into formation. The stallion whirled first, and the mares were still maneuvering to bracket him when Jen got to him. *"Enough,"* she said loudly, reaching up and bashing the creature on its long nose.

The stallion neighed loudly, half-rearing as it hop-stepped back a bit. It shook its head and seemed to blink in surprise. The mares' eyes were wide, and all five creatures' wings were fluttering, banging against each other.

"Enough," Jen repeated, putting her hands on her hips. "This is *my* village, you understand that? We have *rules* here, and you haven't followed them. You will *leave.* Got it?"

Sam's eyes were wide in astonishment, and she was vaguely aware of Vamir rapidly flipping through a book. "Sam," he said urgently, holding the book up to her. "You have to go in there!"

"What?" Sam asked, her eyes still on Jen and the pegasi.

"Look!" Vamir insisted.

Sam tore her eyes away from the scene before her and scanned the line of text Vamir was pointing at. Her eyebrows scrunched together. "I don't get it."

The elf rolled his eyes. "Yes, you do. Even Prudence gets it. That's why she's frowning at you all the time, she comes from a very—"

"No, Prudence and I talked. We're good," Sam insisted, confused. "She—" Sam stopped as understanding dawned. "Oh." Then her eyebrows rose. *"Oh."* An expression of grim determination settled over her face, and she began marching toward Jen.

"I don't get it, either," Warren said.

Vamir read from the book. "A pegasus can only be controlled or intimidated by a spirit bigger than its own."

"Ah," Warren said, nodding slowly. Then he blinked. "I still don't get it."

"Sam and Jen," Leota said gently. "They're. . . like a single soul, split between two bodies. When they come together, when they're thinking together. . . they're far bigger than a single spirit."

"Oh."

Sam had reached Jen's side, and as she stepped into place beside her, the entire world seemed to *thunk* into place. Without looking, she *knew* where every one of the other villagers was—down to the children. And she could *sense* the pegasi with more than just her eyes—and nose. She could feel the walls of the village surrounding them, feel the trees growing in the center of the green. She could even sense the subtle magic that was already regrowing the grass the giant pests had eaten.

The stallion whickered softly, suddenly uncertain. It swung its head left and right, looking for support from the mares, but they'd sensed it too, and had all taken a cautious step back.

Out of the corner of her eye, Sam thought she saw Jen smile.

"This place is ours," the constable said politely but firmly. "You and your pack get."

"She's committed to not being violent here," Sam added. "But you brought that in." She could sense the pegasi hesitating, suddenly unsure of themselves, their earlier arrogance drained away. "You're taking advantage of her peaceful nature. Me? I'm new here." She tapped Nailbiter's hilt. "I'm a bit less committed to the non-violence thing, see? You're beautiful, but you're also disgusting. You have to go."

West, the pub—the village?—whispered. *Follow the new king.*

Sam frowned. *What new king—oh. Right.* "Now as it happens," she continued smoothly, "I happen to know of a settlement with a lot more space. They. . . probably could use something to attract new people, and you lot are certainly attrac-tive." *Until someone gets to know you.* "I'd be happy to show you the way."

"Sam—" Jen started quietly.

"I got this," Sam said confidently.

Jen hesitated, and then nodded. Sam could feel the synergy between them, still, and could feel Jen's trust.

The stallion considered it, and then huffed. Sam took it as agreement. "Let me get my horse."

"Darby!" she heard Warren yell as he thudded off toward the stable at a run.

"Come on," Sam said, turning. Jen pivoted next to her, and the pegasi fell in behind them, the stallion in the lead and the mares following single-file. Everyone scrambled to clear the main gateway, and as Sam and Jen passed through it, Jen stepped off to one side.

"It's a hard day's ride and the sun's almost down," Jen cautioned.

"I'll get them pointed in the right direction and come straight back," Sam said. "We don't have any other horses and Hersin won't carry double." Sam felt oddly confident and at peace, in a way she hadn't felt since. . . *Leeta,* she realized. But the memories of her former shieldmate no longer brough sadness. There was still a soreness there, like a healed bone that still ached in the cold, but. . . there was a calmness behind it, a much-needed acceptance.

Darby was leading a hastily saddled Hersin out into the road. Sam patted the horse, pleased to see that his coat was glossy. "You've put on some weight in your retirement," she chuckled as she swung into the saddle. Darby backed away, his eyes wide as the pegasi followed Sam past the Weary Head and out the west gate.

"Be back soon," she called over her shoulder.

epilogue

. . .

THE SUN WAS PEEKING over the western horizon when Sam rode wearily back into the village.

Everyone had turned out to meet her—even old Knodalon was perched on his bench in front of the storehouse.

"Any trouble?" Jen asked as Sam dismounted and handed the reins over to a sleepy-looking Darby.

Sam shook her head. "No, they were as gentle as palfreys. You know, I think they just wanted someplace to feel safe. Small wonder this place attracted them."

"And Cragg and his people?"

"I didn't go that far. Got maybe halfway and the pegasi started acting excited. They took off past me, nearly at a gallop. I imagine Cragg and his people will be impressed by them, provided they don't try to attack them."

Jen stepped forward and pulled Sam into a tight embrace. "Thank you," she said quietly into Sam's ear.

"You're welcome," Sam replied softly.

They pulled back and smiled at each other. Over Jen's shoulder, Sam could see Leota—supported by Warren—grinning. Even Prudence was wearing a satisfied smile.

Sam felt a prodding in her mind and sighed. "Feels like a full day is coming."

"Everyone back to work," Jen barked cheerfully. "We serve all!"

"Except pegasi," Sam chuckled, shaking her head as she walked toward her pub.

gallery

. . .

Darby

Nate

Minnie

Jen

Makota

Calder

the Dryads

Warren

Vamir

a Pegasus

Knodalon

Galhani

Leota

Dexter

Cole & daughters

Alred

Prudence

Tyran

Lucy

Dardred

about the author

Don Jones spent two decades writing tech books before he finally penned his first sci-fi novella, *A History of the Galactic War.* His well-reviewed and award-winning novels span fantasy and science fiction, with a focus on world building and relatable characters.

Connect, get free novels and short stories, and learn about upcoming releases by visiting Don's author website at DonJones.com.